North Pond Dawn

by

David Roddy

SBS Press

Library of Congress Control Number: 2005924590
ISBN 0-9767539-0-1

SBS Press
P.O. Box 738
Milford, Massachusetts 01757-0738
www.sbspress.com

Printed in the U.S.A. by
Morris Publishing
3212 East Highway 30
Kearney, NE 68847
1-800-650-7888

For Song Bok Soon

Foreword

Several years ago, David Roddy was one of the most insightful telecommunications and Internet analysts in the world. In frequent appearances in the international press, on national television, and on radio, he was able to summarize issues quickly and focus on the implications for business and consumers.

"Cellular phones will eventually surpass traditional telephone networks as the convenience of mobility becomes apparent."
David Roddy, *BusinessWeek*

"The Internet introduces a whole new world of transactions as consumers and business look for new ways to save money."
David Roddy, *Wall Street Journal*

"Competition from cable TV companies to provide high speed connections will put increasing pressure on telephone companies to lower prices."
David Roddy, *CNN Headline News*

"Government agencies will move quickly to allow new competitors into the rapidly growing communications industry."
David Roddy, *New York Times*

But despite the accuracy of his forecasts regarding telecom and Internet developments over the last decade, David could not have anticipated the events described in this book. Read on.

Jack Smith
Washington, D.C.
September 2005

North Pond Dawn

Pocono Medical Center

Unaware that I was in serious danger, I raced through the winding roads of rural Pennsylvania toward the SkyTop Lodge Conference Center where I was scheduled to give a keynote address the next day. At midnight, I stopped at a deserted 7-11 convenience store to buy something to give me energy. As I walked in, I began to feel dizzy. The half-asleep clerk said,

"You look wasted, man."

I was too tired to argue. I was wearing my casual clothes rather than a suit since I did not have to meet anybody when I got to the hotel — tan Dockers pants, a light blue dress shirt, and a dark blue cashmere sweater. So I thought I looked respectable, but he must have seen something in my eyes.

I bought an Italian submarine sandwich and a regular Coke, hoping to keep awake long enough to make it for the last half hour.

"Have a nice night."

"You too," I answered without much enthusiasm.

Even with five No-Doz, it had been a struggle to stay awake during the six-hour trip from Harvard Square in Cambridge — my body seemed to be getting weaker and weaker.

By the time I got to the hotel in the heart of the Pocono Mountains, I was exhausted. I slowly walked into the lobby and sat down. The night clerk was guarding a magnificent oak-paneled atrium with a huge picture window, and a luxury hotel lobby with leather furniture.

"You must be David Roddy. You're the last one to check in … I've been waiting for you. Welcome to our hotel."

"Thanks, the drive took longer than I thought."

She continued as she checked me in, "I've seen you before … on TV talking about the Internet and telephone companies."

"Oh, you did, that's nice."

"I'll have someone take care of your car and luggage."

I leaned back in a comfortable armchair waiting.

"Thank you so much."

The doorman parked the car and picked up my suitcase.

I was so tired I could hardly move. My whole body seemed heavy and drained of energy — it was a struggle just to follow the doorman to the elevator and into my room. I was ready to fall asleep.

But when I took off my shirt, I became frightened to see bruises on many parts of my body. Without hitting anything, they appeared on my legs, arms, and even on my back. Plus, my lower lip was bleeding slightly for some unknown reason. It didn't appear to be from anything normal like cracked chapped lips.

It seemed unwise to just go to bed so I went into the shower and sat down in the tub letting the water try to soothe me. But the bruise on my left arm kept growing and growing right before my eyes — it didn't hurt but it scared me.

I knew a few people at the conference, but they would be asleep by now … anyway they would not be much help with my problems.

For the first time in my life, I went to the lobby and asked to go to the nearest hospital emergency room. I guess I was scared of the unknown.

––––––––––

The Pocono Medical Center seemed designed as a quick stop for vacationers from New York or for elderly people on Medicare — it wasn't what you'd call a large university research medical facility. The emergency room was sparse, with a half dozen beds cordoned off by curtains.

Nicole, the nurse in charge of me, stuck a needle in my left arm for a blood test and took my body temperature, heart rate, and blood pressure. I think I was in stall thirteen but I ignored that kind of thing at the time. The guy in the next stall had just come from a barroom fight where his opponent had gashed his face.

After an hour or so, my blood and urine test results were available and a series of doctors on call came by to puzzle at me and ask me questions and then leave again.

Finally, the night resident in charge of internal medicine, Dr. Tom Edwards, came by with some paperwork to sign.

"Did you really drive from Harvard Square tonight? That's six hours of driving."

"Yes, but I was really tired by the end of the trip. I tried to eat something to give me energy and I took a bunch of No-Doz pills too."

"What brings you here all the way down from Cambridge?"

"I have to attend a conference and give a speech later today. Hopefully, you can give me something to fix me up quickly."

"How much biology and medicine do you know?" he asked.

"Well, I have a Ph.D. in Economics but I never studied biology and in my fifty-four years, have almost never gone to doctors, so I am pretty un-informed." I smiled.

He explained, "Hemoglobin is carried by the red blood cells to distribute oxygen to the rest of your body and take away the carbon dioxide. A usual level for a male is 14."

"The problem with your blood is that your hemoglobin level is only 6. I've never seen a level so low. It indicates severe anemia. You should be exhausted, short of breath, dizzy, light-headed, essentially unable to function normally."

"What about the bruises on my body?"

"Well, you need at least two pints of blood just to keep going while we do further tests to figure that out."

The doctor seemed serious and concerned.

"Your blood is pretty sick."

After I signed the forms, he disappeared and Nicole showed up with a plastic bag of red blood. I had never gotten a blood transfusion before so I was pretty scared. I never did like shots or blood tests, indeed I generally avoided doctors and medical exams. Other than being slightly overweight with a little higher than normal cholesterol, I was pretty healthy.

Surprisingly, the procedure went fine — it was more like sticking a needle in my left arm and dripping some bags of red liquid into my body. It took an hour or so per pint so I listened to the situations of the other emergency patients … a possible heart attack, severe stomach pains, and the gashed face.

It was hard to believe that I was in a hospital emergency room with other sick people. What a difference from the luxury hotel room where I was supposed to be!

Nicole's bubbly voice made the early morning hours pass quickly. She was four months pregnant.

"Baby names are Emma if it's a girl, and Aaron if it's a boy. The baby will probably have blonde hair since that's the way the genes turn out. I will only work ten hours a week after the baby's here. My husband is a distributor for Frito-Lay. They are doing quite well now even though the economy is slow. I guess everyone still eats Fritos and potato chips."

Her voice was soothing but I started to worry what was wrong with my blood and how to handle my speech later that day.

"By the way, what are you doing out here in the Poconos anyway?" she asked.

"Well, I have to give a speech about the Internet and the telephone industry over at a big conference at the SkyTop Lodge this weekend. I'm an international expert on this subject and people from around the world are coming to listen and ask questions, that kind of thing. Actually, I spend a lot of time explaining my ideas on CNN, Nightly Business Report, and the NewsHour with Jim Lehrer."

"Oh my mother watches that show religiously. She likes it because they don't let the various guests get into big fights."

"Yeah, it's pretty good. I just hope that you guys can get me fixed up in time to go over to the conference and give my talk later today."

"We'll see what the doctor says."

Eventually about 5 am, Dr. Edwards came by with a report.

"Something is dangerously wrong in your blood. Nobody can really function with a hemoglobin level of 6 — like I said earlier, light-headed, no strength, no energy, constantly short of breath. Something very serious caused this low of a level. We are moving you up to a regular hospital room so that a specialist can look at you later today."

He disappeared quickly. I said goodbye to Nicole and they wheeled me to the fifth floor to get some sleep. Unfortunately, the upstairs patient area in the hospital had a unique design that broadcast all of the talk and noises of the nurses' station throughout the patients' rooms. With the doors open, I was forced to listen to their chatter and laughter. I knew I needed some rest but that was impossible under the conditions.

I could feel the stress building inside of me like the calm period before a summer storm. I lay awake in the dark, hoping that further tests would show no serious complications. I said to myself, 'No problemo — everything is going to be fine.'

But I was starting to worry as I waited for daylight.

On Friday morning, after the nurses took X- rays and completed a variety of other tests, it was clear that I would not make it over to the Sky Top Lodge. I called over to the conference sponsors and told them I would miss my speech because I was over at the hospital. They were sympathetic and curious. I promised a report later in the weekend.

Time passed so slowly while I waited for more test results. While I lay in the bed, I couldn't do a thing … it was as if I were paralyzed.

Eventually, Dr. Edwards came by to talk about what they knew so far.

"Ok, we have a specialist coming in tomorrow afternoon, but I can give you a little information now. Since we have only done preliminary tests, we can't commit to any particular diagnosis. But, there are a lot of symptoms that make your condition look like a form of cancer called Multiple Myeloma, where your bone marrow produces a continuous stream of plasma cells which basically interfere with the rest of your blood's activities. This is consistent with the other test results and would explain the low hemoglobin level. Keep in mind this is only a tentative diagnosis."

"What???"

"Cancer???"

"As I said, we don't know yet exactly what's going on. Let's wait until tomorrow for more details."

"Please doctor, tell me more! What did you say? Multiple Myeloma? I never heard of that disease before, what are you talking about? I've been healthy all my life. I'm really exhausted right now, so maybe the blood test is all fouled up. That's probably what happened."

He didn't respond to my claim.

"I've called in the local cancer expert who will come to see you on Saturday afternoon, so please relax and let's wait for him to evaluate the information."

I was stunned and terrified as he left the room. I was in a panic.

Cancer? That can't be right. As a non-smoker, it never occurred to me that I might be susceptible.

"No way! Not me!" I was almost shouting out loud.

Terrifying thoughts went through my mind that Friday afternoon. It's not like a cavity or a broken arm … this could change my whole life! No, It can't be right!

But, if what Dr. Edwards said is true, what should I do?

What if?

I had no room for cancer in my life. My son Dan needs me. I must still do a lot for him, and my daughter Amy too, and what about my job? I couldn't stop worrying. If all this turns out to be true, it is much more than a disaster!

Despite the shock of the diagnosis, I was glad about one thing — I was all alone now. Without family and friends, I could try to figure all this out before things really get out of control. At least they don't have to mope around the hospital and say kind things.

————

Friday evening, the resident minister at the hospital, Chaplain Christine, came by to see me since I was on the list of those with new and serious medical information. She was a chubby friendly Canadian with a ready smile and a fervent interest in me because I might have a serious cancer.

We walked around the hospital floor that formed a square with about 20 rooms on each side around the nurses' station.

"People tend to get angry when they find out they have cancer for the first time. How do you feel David?"

I shrugged, not knowing what to say.

She gave me a warm smile and continued.

"It could be a lot different future than you expected."

"You know Christine, I've been so busy calling people to say that I'm in the hospital and couldn't go to my conference. It just hasn't occurred to me that this is real yet."

As usual, I tried to hide what I was really thinking. She continued.

"You might not have that rest and enjoyment of retirement that many people look forward to."

"Well," I answered hopefully, "It still does not seem so serious. I haven't really focused on cancer at all. Besides, I'm not sure that I'm really sick — I feel fine after the new blood."

But that was a lie. Although she was trying to be nice to me, I was starting to feel lost and distant. All of a sudden her pager beeped and she said she had to go to the emergency room to counsel relatives of an accident victim whose life had ended prematurely.

"Talk to you later," I managed weakly.

The walk back to my room was painful. I felt as if I was being dragged there by mysterious forces because I had nowhere else to go. My mind was urging me to head for the front door and forget the whole episode. But my body slowly trudged back to an uncomfortable hospital bed and a nurse waiting to take my blood pressure.

On Saturday I managed to get on the Internet with my laptop computer using the hospital phone line and an 800 number to my company's Internet Service Provider. I spent the morning browsing the Internet for information on the telephone industry. Then I visited most of the sites in my favorites list: the New York Times, Korean language tutorials, and European travel destinations. It was clearly a case of avoidance.

People sometimes say that time flies, especially when we are doing exciting things ... but now, time seemed to stand still. I was trapped and had nowhere to go. I was waiting and waiting and waiting.

I finally looked up Multiple Myeloma on the Google search page. It was sort of interesting. I just wished it weren't about me. What I learned was that the plasma cells — which come from your bone marrow and form antibodies to fight disease — somehow forget their usual behavior and start multiplying abnormally. Eventually they crowd out the good parts of your blood, seriously damage your bones, and interfere with your immune system.

The most common word used with Multiple Myeloma was 'incurable.' It seemed impossible that my blood could have such a thing. Except for a slightly elevated cholesterol level, it had always been fine before. The tests were probably wrong. I went back to the European travel site again after that and looked for nice places to go with my friend Shin some day.

The love of my life, Shin Be Sun, is a marvelous combination of calm and fire, delight and persistence, wisdom and youth. With dark black hair like most Koreans, she is fairly athletic at 125 pounds and a little over 5 feet 6. She easily looks 30 or so yet she has two grown daughters who graduated from college several years ago.

She gives off rays of confident inspiration that are catching to anyone nearby. She is the smartest, warmest, kindest and most enthusiastic person I have ever known. To me she is an angel from heaven more precious than sunshine.

I have loved her dearly ever since I first met her four years ago when we were both visiting Japan. At the time I was giving a speech about the Internet to one of the largest cellular phone companies in Japan. It was a one week trip and that was my second visit to Tokyo.

After my speech, I decided to look around this exotic city, but my problem was that nobody seemed to speak much English.

Of course at the conference they had translators, but outside of the hotel everything was in Japanese. I decided to take a day-long tour around the city to cure my loneliness and learn more about East Asia. Shin was on the bus alone, studiously writing Japanese along with Korean translations on a paper that she held in her lap. At first, I was so happy to meet her because her English was so good. But as she talked, it seemed that she was casting a magic spell on me.

Her life story was fascinating ... an almost unbelievable sequence of struggle and success. When she was young in Korea, she had no money to go to high school, but had to go to work instead so her brothers and sister could continue to study. She worked twelve hours a day seven days a week at a textile factory for ten years until she got married.

But despite the difficulties, she said that she had never felt sad or depressed ... there was no time for such luxuries. She worked hard, supported her family, and studied on her own to catch up to all her church friends who went to school. She never shied from responsibility even if it meant that she had to sacrifice her own plans.

After ten years, she quit the textile mill, got married and had two daughters. Unfortunately, she had married the oldest son ... in Korea that meant that she had to take care of ten other relatives, cooking, cleaning, and washing clothes for them. It's a strange system that I have never completely understood.

Over the years, she sent her two daughters to the best university in Korea, taught herself excellent English, and traveled to many countries of the world by herself.

While we talked on the bus, she clearly explained to me the differences between written Japanese, Chinese, and Korean. Since I have always been interested in foreign languages, I found myself becoming enchanted by her. But even more than technical knowledge, her conversations always seem to contain some brilliant thread of quiet wisdom. Plus, she is always so happy and optimistic. As I began to get to know her, I thought, 'I have been looking for this kind of woman all my life and here she is.'

So, for the last of couple of years my main goal has been to encourage her to stay with me all of the time. I asked her to get married several times, but her answer was always that she needs more time to take care of her two daughters who are still in Korea. Even though they are grown up, for her they are still her children — and she felt that she had to take care of them until they get married. She urged me to wait for a couple of years.

So for now, I was happy to see her whenever she comes to the United States. During these visits, we learn a lot about each other, laughing and talking about our past experiences and future dreams. Most of all, we just spend time enjoying life together.

The cancer expert for the region came by on Saturday afternoon. Dr. Joe Anders was tall and quiet and his deep voice exhibited an easy authority that was unarguable when he spoke. He had his own hematology / oncology practice locally and was associated with the Memorial Sloan-Kettering Cancer Center in New York City.

He was direct and to the point.

"I looked at your test results and X-rays this morning. You probably have stage 3 Multiple Myeloma cancer. We haven't had much success dealing with this kind of cancer so far. And stage 3 is pretty advanced. Overall, the median survival rate is one to two years. So half of the patients live less than that, the other half several years more."

I was stunned. My brain went numb. I couldn't respond … not even to ask questions. The doctor stood awkwardly looking blankly out the window. Terror raced through my mind.

This can't be right.

I knew something was wrong in my body ... but not death.

No! No! No!

One or two years?

Oh God! Please help me! Not now!

This was the first time the word cancer and death had been linked to me. I had never thought about how long I would live before. I guess I had assumed that cancer meant you get chemotherapy, lose your hair, have nausea, and then the cancer goes into remission. This new assessment sounded far more dangerous than I had imagined.

"Are you sure about all this?"

My voice was weak and hollow ... almost unrecognizable.

"The only way to confirm the diagnosis is to do a bone marrow biopsy — a procedure where we take some bone marrow from your hip bone and look at the Myeloma cells under a microscope. The survival rate information I mentioned is not exact but it gives you an idea of what we know from past cases. This is not breast cancer or colon cancer where we have better experience. Myeloma is pretty tough to handle."

Oh God! This is it! I have a deadly cancer called Multiple Myeloma.

I'm dying ... 'incurable.'

'Blood cancer!'

'Two years to live!'

I had never considered such a fate before. I was totally frozen by the shock of the verdict. This is worse then life in prison, I thought, remembering episodes from the movies. How can I accept that he is talking about me and not another patient in the next room? But this is real life, not a dream. It's not a movie or a book. It's my life.

Wait, this can't be about me! What am I going to do now? Suddenly, I was embarrassed by my silence.

"Doc, when can you do the biopsy to confirm the diagnosis?"

12

"How about the day after tomorrow? You just try to get some rest until then. The nurses will get you ready and we will meet in the operating room first thing Monday morning. By the way, they said you are from the Boston area. That's good. I have my assistant looking for a contact at the Dana Farber Cancer Institute there. They have some of the best doctors in the world working on Myeloma."

"Thanks, that's great." What a stupid thing to say, but it was a verbal habit that I generally used in order to be friendly. Further discussion with the doctor seemed almost pointless. When he left, I wondered if this was typical of his conversations with terminally ill patients.

Despite the cancer news, my near term problem was more immediate. I had to get in touch with Shin at her sister's house in North Carolina and tell her not to come to Cambridge yet. Unfortunately, I did not have her sister's phone number. And Shin and I did not always talk when we had a set plan.

She had gone to Korea to see her daughters and visit old friends. On the way back she brought her sister's elderly mother-in-law to North Carolina for her first visit to the United States. Then she planned to come and visit me in Harvard Square.

I was supposed to pick her up at the airport in Boston on Monday. Now I started to panic since Shin would be at the airport wondering where I was. At about that time I would be in surgery getting a bone marrow biopsy.

Chaplain Christine stuck her head in to see how my meeting with the cancer expert had gone.

"What's the news?"

"I guess I have a very serious cancer. I'm still in shock. I don't really believe that I'm talking about myself."

"Oh, David, I'm so sorry to hear that. Please let me know whenever you need to talk."

"Well, Christine, I do have one problem that I'm trying to deal with. Do you remember that I said I'm going to have my friend visit from Korea?"

"Yes, you mean Shin right?"

"Yeah, I'm supposed to meet her on Monday. But now, I have to tell her not to come to yet. Unfortunately, I don't know how to contact her because I haven't found a way to get her sister's phone number in North Carolina. Any ideas?"

"Well, I'm not sure. I'll say a prayer about it ... maybe that will help. I'll be back later."

Then she disappeared, and I was left alone to deal with the mysterious poison in my blood. And a lifetime suddenly destroyed in just a matter of days.

I searched the Internet but still could find no phone listing for Shin's sister. Although we did email frequently, it was likely that she would not be checking it from her sister's house. Finally, an idea struck. I would email her daughter, Ejin, in Korea and get the phone number that way. Fortunately, her daughter was checking email and promptly emailed back the phone number in North Carolina. I breathed a sigh of relief. Almost as if that phone number somehow solved all these new problems.

On Sunday afternoon, I tried to plan what I would say to Shin that night on the phone. This effort was sad and depressing. I knew that cancer was not my fault. But it had sure wrecked my future. I was trying to convince her to stay with me and live with me and eventually marry me. But who would marry a guy with a lifetime of one or two years? And what would the financial picture look like with this new disease? A massive explosion had just destroyed all my hopes and dreams.

Should I tell her directly about the cancer news, or would it be too much for her? Or should I wait until she comes to Boston

and tell her when I see her? My mind went back and forth —
what is the best way to tell her? I guess if I were her, I would
want to know everything right a way. I was sweating and my
hands were shaking. I was starting to panic.

I guess I should tell her the whole story directly since she
does not like to get the news in pieces. It would definitely be a
shock — one hour counting on coming to visit Harvard Square
and play at the area golf courses, the next hour having to deal
with someone who is dying of cancer with future plans in total
disarray.

My heart was breaking when we started to talk on the phone.
She sounded normal.

"Hi David, how are you doing? I'm so excited to be coming
to Boston again to see you and play golf."

As usual, her voice bubbled with enthusiasm.

"How was the Friday speech at the telecom conference in the
Poconos?"

"Well ..."

"Guess what? I've taken a lot of golf lessons when I was in
Korea this time, so I am getting really good. Ta-da! So will you
come and pick me up at the airport?"

My brain froze. It was impossible for me to talk.

"Let me call you back Shin."

I hung up the phone.

At this point, I thought, how could I tell her that I'm dying of
cancer? I still couldn't believe it myself — but if I didn't tell her
now, she would keep asking me what's wrong. I can't pretend as
if nothing has happened.

I punched in each number slowly again.

"Hi Shin, I need to tell you something important. Could I talk
a couple of minutes?"

"Of course David, what's wrong?'

"Actually I got to the hotel in the Poconos on Thursday night but I never made it to the conference."

"What do you mean, you never gave the speech ... is something wrong?"

She seemed to want to know all the news now, and maybe she is strong enough to absorb this disaster. But I still hesitated to tell her. I had thought about this all day, but I was still unsure how to proceed. Sooner or later I must let her know anyway. Yet it seemed too devastating for a phone call. But I had no choice. So I continued.

"Well, right now I'm in the hospital."

She was frantic.

"What happened? I thought you called here to confirm that you were going to pick me up at the airport. When did you go to the hospital? What's wrong? Please tell me what is going on."

My voice trembled.

"Shin I'm so sorry to give this news to you on the phone."

I was about to cry. All of a sudden, I felt so vulnerable.

"When I got to the hotel at midnight on Thursday, I started feeling very sick. So I took an ambulance to the emergency room at the Pocono Medical Center which is about a half hour from the hotel. That is where I am now. After many tests, the doctor now says that I have a form of cancer that is quite bad."

"Oh no! oh no! What do you mean 'bad cancer'?"

"The doctor says that it is pretty severe and has affected all of my blood. It is called Multiple Myeloma and goofs up my blood cells and bone marrow in very dangerous ways."

"Oh no, oh no! This can't be true!"

I could feel her shock as she absorbed the news about cancer. It was like she had driven into a sudden blizzard on the highway that makes everything totally white ... with no orientation or sense of balance.

"Do you remember the mysterious bruises that appeared on my arms now and then? And the shortness of breath trying to walk fast? Those were both symptoms of the cancer that I have."

"Oh David! It can't be right! I don't know what to say! Maybe the tests were mixed up in the lab. Maybe it's only a temporary problem that can be fixed with a week's worth of medicine. I will check out to see if any kind of oriental herb medicine might help you."

That moment we both cried on the phone for several minutes. All I could hear was her quiet sobbing.

"I am hopeful my dear Shin, but the doctor said it's really cancer and it won't go away that easily. They say that I might live only two years or so. There are ways to treat it with medication, but mostly the drugs just prolong life a little longer."

"Oh no! Oh my God!"

Still in shock, she asked, "Did you talk to your kids Dan and Amy? Not waiting for an answer, she continued.

"Oh dear David! Who is going to take care of you? And what are you going to do with Dan? When you told me how you take care of your son, it was a wonderful story. What a great father you are! But..."

Dan is one of the friendliest and most delightful sons you will ever meet. He is twenty-eight now and works at the library and volunteers at a nearby hospital and a local food bank. He was born three months early, but he has made tremendous progress since the medical complications he had early in his life. But, he has only a few friends and no one to rely on except his family. So I and my ex-wife have helped him do things ever since he was born. He needs extra care for some things — for others he is just fine. With help, he got an Associates Degree from a local college. And he is extremely proud of his rather large collection of classic video game systems and over a thousand games. He and I play many of them frequently together — but my favorite is still the Atari 2600 version of Space Invaders.

Shin's voice was full of stress.

"David, have you told Dan yet?"

"Not yet, this is not the kind of thing that he would easily understand. I would like to visit him in person to tell him what's going on. And I talked to Amy yesterday to say that I am in the hospital but no details yet."

"David, what should I do for you? Tell me, how can I help you now? How do you feel?"

"I don't feel physically sick, but I do feel like I'm stuck inside of a tornado with everything flying around me. I have no control of anything and I don't know where I will land. I feel like a huge disappointment to you."

I was getting more and more depressed. How can I talk about a happy future with her when in reality, my dreams are crashing to the floor like a broken window?

But her response put perspective in a way that only she can do. Her voice tone changed. She seemed to be absorbing the severity of the situation.

"Listen, my dear David. In all my lifetime, I saw lots of miracles happen to me. As you know, I was born in a poor country with no money to go to high school. I worked constantly to buy food and clothes for my brothers and sister. You cannot imagine how difficult my early life was. But now I have finally achieved success. So David do not give up yet! Are you listening?"

I was holding the phone hopelessly.

"Yes Shin, I'm here."

She continued.

"I already did what I wanted to do in my lifetime … well, almost everything. Please let me help you now. You are not a disappointment or anything like that at all! You are the most innocent person I ever met, you are such a good man, and a great father. Dan needs you and I also need you so please be strong. It's not your fault that you have cancer, you know that."

I interrupted her … I couldn't bear to continue talking until I had some idea of a plan for the future.

"Shin can you stay at your sister's a couple more weeks while I figure out how this disaster will affect my life?"

"David I understand what you are telling me. But please listen a little bit more."

The nurse came in to take my temperature but I waved at her to come back later. Shin continued.

"Two is better than one right? So together we should make sure that this cancer is only a little bit of a glitch in our lives. Let me come to see you so we can confront this evil disease together. Let me be with you and take care of you right away. Don't tell me to wait. I must come now. Let me make another miracle in my life again. In Korea, I have no one to take care of now so I don't need to go back there that much. As I told you, I am already free from my family and my obligations there are almost done."

Numbness took over again and I could not think or talk. My heart was breaking and I just couldn't continue. So I tried to hang up the phone.

"Shin, I have to go now, the nurse is going to give me some more blood."

But she continued, "Ok, be optimistic. We have each other to confront this tragedy together. Now you should know that your lifetime on earth is much more valuable than ever before. There is no time for being disappointed or depressed. Your life is even more precious than you know. Don't ever think that you are alone. This cancer will not destroy you. Let me say this directly. I am going to stick with you no matter what happens from now on."

My brain started to spin. What does that mean? Does she mean that she will live with me now? Making my dreams about her come true just as I find out that incurable cancer is leaving me with only two years to live? Is this a comfort or a tragedy?

'I will stick with you no matter what.' Were her words a blessing or a sad reminder?

She kept talking. "Hang in there David. And please be strong for me. You and I must conquer this cancer. From now on, you are the only person in the world that I have to take care of. So we will beat this cancer together and be the winners in our lives."

"I'll try," I said, in a weak attempt to be enthusiastic."

"Please don't tell me not to come now!"

We arranged to meet in Harvard Square later that week.

"See you so very soon, my dearest darling Shin."

When I hung up the phone, I was terrified. What could be the new plan for our life together? My only hope at the moment was to believe that I would wake up from a bad dream, meet Shin at the airport, play golf with her, and get back to work. How could I see her now and be so helpless? I have never ever been in that position before.

On Monday morning, I got ready for the bone marrow biopsy at the Pocono Medical Center. One nurse described it as sticking a corkscrew into my hipbone and pulling out some bone chips and the inner marrow. Since I had always shied away from pain, I told Dr. Anders to give me medication so I wouldn't feel a thing. It worked. One moment, I saw the doctor unwrapping his surgical instruments, then all of a sudden, I woke an hour later after the biopsy and they wheeled me back to my hospital room.

One of the nurses had kindly moved me out of the noisy part of the floor into a private room area with a nice view of the trees in the Pocono mountains. I was still groggy from the medicine so I just went back to sleep. The doctor needed to develop and study the films, so I would have to wait until Tuesday to get definitive results. But I already knew.

At the same time, his assistant was busy locating the right referral contact at the Dana Farber Cancer Institute. Luckily it was located only a half hour from my Harvard Square apartment. On the Internet, I found that they had a special center for Multiple Myeloma care and the reports indicated that they were working on various new drug therapies that could extend life somewhat beyond the original two year prediction. And some of the treatments did not involve losing hair or vomiting or radiation.

On Monday afternoon, Dr. Edwards stopped by as he was checking on the condition of all the patients on the floor. He referred all my cancer questions to Dr. Anders, so I volunteered that psychologically I felt pretty good — maybe I would look for one last great accomplishment to achieve before my health got really bad.

His response was mildly critical.

"You've got a Ph.D. in Economics, that's already a great success. Why not go to that nice restaurant you always wanted to? It would also be a good time to renew personal relationships that have fallen by the wayside in your fast-paced consulting career. Calm down the ambition a bit."

"But I only have two years to live. I have to work harder to leave behind something important."

"Don't fool yourself. This deadly cancer is serious — it will take a lot of time and attention. The medications to control it will also make you feel weak. You won't have the time and strength that you are used to. You will have to focus on slowing down and letting your body dictate activities."

At the time, I had the new blood that made me feel physically great and my brain was ready to make arrangements and get back to work. Besides, Shin is now coming to stay and take care of me.

So I thought his message was short-sighted, almost urging me to give up and admit defeat. I knew that I would have to struggle to survive and succeed. And I did not know exactly how I would take care of Shin. But give up? Not me.

Yet the cancer news eventually began to weigh very heavy. Monday dinner featured summer tomatoes that Nicole had carried in from her garden. Shin eats tomatoes a half-dozen at a time. Once when a friend offered her a slice of one to put on a sandwich, she was shocked, 'What are they saving them for? They are beautiful and full of vitamins.' As I stared at the red softness, I wondered how much longer I would be able to eat tomatoes with Shin.

Monday night I couldn't sleep. Maybe it was the morning nap after the biopsy, maybe it was the stress of the newly acquired information. I tried to relax. My mind wandered to my trips with Shin in Europe.

She has a delightfully stubborn nature that is so refreshing and motivating. Once she went with me to Paris to look around when I had a business trip there. When we arrived at the airport, I started to call around for hotels because this was peak tourist season and Paris hotels would most likely be full. She stopped me from calling. 'Don't waste your time. Just be spontaneous. Let's go downtown and look around. We'll find something.'

This made me nervous — perhaps she was not familiar with the summer tourist crowds in Paris and last minute reservations. I was trying to impress her with my organizational skills and I felt complications ahead.

We found a taxi, headed downtown, and got out at a major hotel. As I expected, the hotel was full. With our luggage on the curb, we looked around a beautiful section of Paris that totally amazed Shin. I was getting agitated. All of a sudden, she pointed out an Avis-rent-a-car sign down the street.

She exclaimed, "That's it! Let's rent a car. Worst case, we could just sleep in it. Better yet, we can travel out in the country-side and find a small hotel that won't be overrun by tourists. Don't worry about a thing. I know what I'm doing."

Since then that phrase has became our playful motto.

She stayed with the luggage and it took about fifteen minutes to get the car. When I got back to pick her up, she said I had the biggest happiest smile on my face that she can ever remember. We drove around Paris that summer evening and ate dinner at an Alsatian restaurant in the university district. I think it was the best Quiche Lorraine that I had ever eaten. Then we headed south past Versailles toward the castles and countryside of the Loire Valley.

We stayed at a small inn with a wonderful view of a famous stone castle built in the Middle Ages. The next day, Shin looked gorgeous in white shorts and a silver t-shirt. Her light yellow-tan skin was so smooth and her black hair was pulled back in a cute pony-tail. The wind-blown wheat fields sparkled golden in the sun. As we drove along, Shin began to sing Korean folk songs and church hymns in her wonderful alto voice.

As we passed a field of red poppies, her voice rang with a freedom and joy that had been trapped inside for years and now was pouring out like a bottle of champagne. My eyes were stunned by her beauty as a feeling of sheer delight took over my body. It was as if I were ten years old awakening on Christmas morning. Her magic wrapped me in an ecstasy that I had not felt in all my life. She was enchanting.

I knew then that I was falling in love.

One of the nice things about this rural hospital was a large menu that you got for each meal and you could order anything that you wanted. I started to eat a lot. I wanted to live. At breakfast, I had scrambled eggs and toast and cereal and fruit.

At lunch, I had chicken salad sandwiches and French fries and beets and chocolate pudding. Supper was fish and rice and asparagus and ice cream. It was as if I thought a lot of good food could cure the poison in my blood.

On Tuesday morning, I had an omelet and French toast. I was waiting to talk with the oncologist, Dr. Anders, to find out the official results of the bone marrow biopsy. The procedure apparently involved looking at the amount of Myeloma cells in the bone marrow under a microscope. He walked in just as I got some syrup on my right hand. I shook hands anyway but was a little embarrassed.

"You definitely have Multiple Myeloma cancer. It is quite advanced, what we would call stage 3. We don't see any bone or kidney damage yet, but you will have to do more tests when you get back to Cambridge. As I said on Saturday, most patients live for one or two years after this point — but newer medicines might make that a little longer."

I had no questions. That was it.

He was gone.

I was dying.

On the trip back to Harvard Square, everything looked greener and nicer after four days in the hospital. Only the funeral homes and cemeteries looked different.

Dealing with Cancer

Summertime in a university town is delightful because the massive crowds are thinned out considerably leaving the permanent residents with a mixture of foreign students studying English and working professionals attending three week specialized seminars. But my condition imposed its own new context. Walking around the bookstores, restaurants, and libraries near Harvard University, it soon became impossible to look at people without feeling jealous. I would see a businessman or a professor or even a graduate student and think, 'Why couldn't I be like them?'

What vicious twist of fate had robbed me of my future with Shin and my successful career as a consultant — all within the last week? The shock was setting in and I was anxious and upset. 'Why me?' I wondered bitterly. I had certainly made mistakes in my life, but nothing to deserve this treatment.

I went over to the Micro-Center computer store on Memorial Drive to look around and cheer myself up. I have been a technology and computer hobbyist since college days so there was always something to play with or investigate there. Yet a mysterious and somber feeling grabbed me as I walked in.

The last time I was here a couple of months ago, I was joking with Shin and dragging her around to look at gadgets she playfully complained about. Back then, the future was bright with hardly a care in the world.

Now everything was totally different — and in a very serious way. This was no simple matter of getting fired or going through a divorce. This was the big kahuna ... life itself, existence, feelings, breathing oxygen, looking at sunsets, waking up in the morning. Shin had once told me 'The difference between life and death is moving and not moving.' I didn't pay much attention at the time. But now ...

I left the store without touring my favorite sections. It seemed that the speed of the change in my situation was more than I could bear.

I found myself repeating this 'the last time I was in this place' nightmare more and more. It was starting to get on my nerves but I didn't seem to have control of what my brain dictated when I walked into a building. It was a constant depressing reminder even when I needed a break to just erase my mind and fall back into the pillows.

———

Even though it was almost the Memorial Day holiday, I was able to get a meeting with a doctor in the Multiple Myeloma group at Dana Farber Cancer Institute on Thursday, while Shin was still on the way here.

A longtime Boston resident, I had heard of the Jimmy Fund for twenty years in the media. This was the name used to raise funds to help find cures for cancer — especially for children. Dana Farber and the Boston Red Sox had been cooperating for the last 50 years and have been credited with raising billions of dollars to help fight this most elusive set of diseases.

The Dana Farber building was located in the middle of a dozen medical schools and hospitals near downtown Boston. Inside, it was decorated with Boston Red Sox souvenirs. It was crowded with patients who had almost every kind of cancer. They were getting blood, giving blood, meeting doctors and nurses, and getting medicine.

Suddenly, I experienced a strange feeling of relief for the first time since I was diagnosed. I thought, 'I'm not the only one who gets cancer. There are a lot of us.' I saw a sign on the bulletin board advertising a meeting of a support group for Multiple Myeloma. It seemed oddly comforting to see my rare illness clearly recognized in a public place.

Dr. Nick Portinari, a short, enthusiastic oncologist from Italy met with me and looked at all the records that Dr. Anders had given to me when I left the Pocono Medical Center. Dr. Portinari had spent time in a variety of cancer hospitals in the United States and was well-known for his expertise in Multiple Myeloma and related blood cancers.

He had just returned from Australia, where he had given a speech on the latest treatment options. In order to be concise, I had summarized what I had learned from Dr. Anders about my condition on a single sheet of yellow paper.

Dr. Portinari was a quick reader ... even upside down. He promptly crossed out the line where I had written 'median time of survival — one to two years.'

"This is wrong ... we have plenty of new treatments. If one doesn't work, we go on to the next one. We have new experimental medicines in clinical trials, established treatments with good track records, and things in the laboratory that should be ready in the next two years. Don't worry. You've got plenty of years left."

"Do I have to do radiation treatments, vomit, and lose my hair?" My question seemed almost trivial in comparison to the life-threatening cancer in my blood.

"No, No. None of these involve that kind of treatment yet."

I breathed a sigh of relief. His optimism was catching and after seven pints of blood in the Poconos and a much higher hemoglobin level, I was feeling better and better. All the health insurance paperwork seemed to be in order so that was a great comfort as well. Only my hip hurt where Dr. Anders had done the biopsy.

One alternative that Dr. Portinari discussed was a clinical trial of a new drug called Compade that was not yet approved by the FDA. Our results would be part of the record eventually submitted to show the effectiveness of the medication. This seemed the most promising so I decided to begin as soon as possible.

But first, another bone marrow biopsy, some X-rays, and then a dialysis-like medical procedure called pheresis to clean my blood before starting the new drug. I asked how effective I would be at work with my new cancer and these treatments. He said "Eighty percent or better, just continue as normal. Go for it." A pretty good Thursday after all.

———

But just when things were looking up, a thirty-mile an hour gust blows through the house slamming all the doors. When I got back to the apartment from the optimistic visit with Dr. Portinari, I had a fed ex letter from my employer, Internet Economics Consulting, saying that I had been placed on 'leave without pay' for medical reasons. So on Tuesday, I learned that I had a deadly cancer — on Thursday, I got fired.

I rushed into the office the next day to talk to Mary, the Human Resources administrator, to try to remedy the situation. I had notified her when I was in the hospital just to make sure that all the proper insurance procedures were being followed. She had passed the information on to IEC headquarters who promptly generated the letter, adjusted the computer, and took away my salary.

"I guess somebody jumped the gun?" I asked.

She was sympathetic since she had been out with cancer before. "I was as shocked as you when I saw the letter from headquarters. We're still adjusting to this new company, IEC, that recently bought us. I checked into this and they said that it was company policy."

"This can't be right. It's impossible. Fire someone two days after they learn they have cancer? I've never heard of such a thing. What a message to send to other employees. What a response to all the calls for a new 'corporate responsibility'. Most of all what happens to my health insurance?"

"I think we can fix this but we have to deal with headquarters to get you back on the payroll. What you need is a letter from your doctor saying that you can go back to work full time including business travel and perform your duties as normal."

"That should be easy to get."

"Oh, headquarters also wants to see evidence that you had health insurance when you started employment with us back in December."

"What? Are they saying that you need existing health insurance in order to sign up for health insurance with a new employer? If this is a national trend, millions of uninsured-unemployed who finally find a job could be in for a nasty surprise."

"I have no idea, but can you dig up any paperwork you have on the health insurance plan that you had?"

"Sure, but it lapsed because I stopped paying the premiums about six months before I joined IEC. So technically, I had no health insurance when I walked in the door. Is headquarters claiming that even though my application was accepted and I have been paying the premiums, that I might not really have health insurance after all?"

"I'm not sure, but anything is possible since we are still trying to conform our benefits program with theirs. They are trying to cut costs and they may have made a separate agreement with the health carrier that we don't fully understand."

Later that day, she checked back.

"IEC headquarters seems to be claiming that they assured the health carrier that everybody who signed up would already have health insurance coming in. Then our health carrier could contact the other company to help pay if there was a case of pre-existing conditions. Unfortunately, they did not tell us, it's not in the company benefits manual, and they did not notify anyone when they signed up for health insurance that a requirement was existing insurance with another company."

"Sounds idiotic to me." But companies have used all kinds of tactics to save money, so I was turning pessimistic.

"I'll do my best," Mary assured me, "but get me the doctor's letter and whatever health insurance paperwork you have as soon as possible."

"Ok, I'll have the letters by the end of the week."

My employer had fired me for getting cancer and was now claiming that the health insurance that I had signed up for and paid for was not really valid. What a company! I became worried and suspicious. This cancer would be a big financial cost and I did not have the money to pay without insurance.

That night I tried to watch television to pass the time, but that strategy back-fired. Every other commercial was advertising retirement plans and wonderful things to do in our old age. But now I would be left without many more years and without much money. I guess it took my mind off the details of the cancer in my blood for a while. But it wasn't very reassuring.

In the meantime, Shin had rented a car and was driving the eighteen-hour trip from North Carolina to Harvard Square. She called from a service area in the middle of the night.

"Hi David, guess where I am?"

"Some motel between here and North Carolina?"

"Nope, I'm still driving. I will be there early in the morning. Hang in there David, I'm coming!" Her voice was full of enthusiasm and confidence.

"By the way, what did the Dana Farber doctor say about your treatment?"

"Good news from the doctor. When you come here I will give you the details. So please go to a motel and sleep so you can drive safely tomorrow."

She ignored my advice, and kept asking questions.

"What kind of good news?"

"I saw a cancer expert named Dr. Portinari. He had more information than I got from the Pocono Medical Center. They have a lot of new medical treatments at Dana Farber that can extend my life much more than what the other doctor mentioned. So please go to a motel and get some rest. I'm in better shape than I thought."

"Oh! Thank God! That is good news. Listen David, I can't rest before I see you. When I get there I'll sleep — I need to see you first. So don't worry about me, I know what I'm doing. Remember? You go to sleep. Now I am the one who is going to take care of you. Good-bye, see you very soon."

My Shin is coming to take care of me! Everything is going to be fine soon. Her wonderful magic was already working on me.

When she arrived early the next morning, we hugged and kissed like never before, the first human loving touch since I had learned of my deadly fate. I was still deeply embarrassed about my newfound helplessness when I first saw her. But her beautiful smile has always drawn a natural reaction from me. She described it, 'Your eyes twinkle and your face scrunches up — just like a boy.'

"My dearest darling, you are here, I'm so sorry, I'm so very sorry."

31

Although it was clearly not a very accurate thing to say, I was still suffering from the feeling that I was somehow letting Shin down by getting this cancer. Almost as if I had dragged her into some complicated and dangerous mission that had gone awry and now there was no easy way for her to call it quits and escape. Perhaps not a sensible feeling, but with all that has happened to me, I didn't seem willing to demand a completely logical treatment from my emotions.

She must have cried a lot on the trip down. Her face was red where she had tried to wipe away the tears. She looked so tired because she had not slept in days. But still she is astonishingly beautiful. And now she breathed a sigh of relief and gave me a great big smile.

"Oh, David, I'm finally here to take care of you. Don't ever say sorry, nothing is your fault, it's not anybody's fault. Let me see you. You look good."

She hugged me tightly again, then she seemed relieved.

"We will get through this. You know what? We will be playing in a sailboat on the lake sooner than you think. And then, I will take you wherever you want to go."

What great confidence she has.

"So tell me everything that has happened ever since this cancer bomb dropped on you."

"I feel great," I said, avoiding her question.

And since I looked about the same in terms of physical appearance as when I had last seen her, it was easy to pay no attention to the strange and invisible difficulties with my blood. We hugged each other again and again. We didn't even realize that our faces were full of tears. Standing there holding hands, we were still not willing to admit that things were tragically different now. When it came to cancer, we didn't really know what to say or how to say it.

I gently managed to guide her into the apartment. She looked around, took a shower, and changed her clothes. I sat on the sofa and relaxed. For the first time in a long time, I felt content ... the love of my life had come to play with me. What more could I ask for?

After she went to bed to get some rest, I watched her perfectly shaped body tremble with tension and relief. How much I had longed for this moment! She was so beautiful and delicate, yet her character was so strong and courageous. I felt somehow safer then ever before.

She fell asleep and I took stock of my predicament.

I love her so dearly more and more, every single day. And I have been trying to convince her to live with me for the last several years. It seemed almost unbearable to wreck our dreams with this desperately bad news about my health.

My original plan was to take care of her, support her, play with her, and give her an opportunity to do whatever she wants to do. I had promised to send her to Harvard University Extension School when I heard her story about how badly she wanted to go to school when she had to work instead. I thought that I would rescue her from the difficulties that she had endured over her lifetime. Now, my heart started to ache because I was bringing her more.

Shin woke up with a start, sensing my worries. She held my hand and began talking gently but strongly.

"You know David, what I believe in God is simple but so powerful. It has helped me survive all the hard times that I have been through."

"No matter what bad things happen to you in your life, do not complain, be upset, or be depressed, and never be sad. The only thing that you have to do to overcome the difficulties is to look for what you still have now and give thanks to God for that."

"That's my prayer. Even if I come up with the worst situation, I know that there will still be things to thank God for. When you are looking for what is good or what you have, then your mind becomes content so that you can focus on what you have to do about the problem before you."

"If I prayed 'Oh please give something to me to solve the problem', it's not going to happen. And even if I said, 'please get rid of David's cancer', it's not going to work right now, I know that. If I pray for a big house or enough money to live, I know that's not going to happen either."

"A request is not a prayer. God will give you what you need … you don't have to ask, God already knows."

Then she laid back and closed her eyes in a peaceful sleep. I went to the living room and rested on the couch, amazed at the clarity of what she had just told me.

———

When she woke up, she was wearing a comfortable blue and brown floor-length dress which included a top as well, sort of a jumper, and a long sleeve soft green sweater. Her walk was confident and hopeful. She seemed to be gaining more and more strength after she had some rest.

"How about a walk to the Charles River — I haven't been there for a while."

"That's a great idea … let's go."

We left the apartment and walked along the streets near Harvard University, smelling the lush green trees and remembering back to last summer when we made frequent trips to Hopkinton State Park to sail on a small lake. I had spent years doing this when I was young, so I was pretty good at it.

Before we got to the river, I persuaded Shin to stop at a Starbucks for a quick coffee. Somehow the wood chairs, pungent smell, and the New York Times combined to give me a sense of security. That was an environment that I knew well.

We talked in a corner while we listened to the smooth sounds of gentle jazz.

"When I was young in Korea, I went to church every Sunday. But that wasn't always a happy moment for me because I was so poor. I prayed and prayed but it never made my life easier. I cried a lot when I felt that God did not answer me. I complained — why am I the only one suffering from all this when all my friends are able to go to school? Why didn't God answer me?"

"After many years of desperation, finally God gave me the understanding to make me realize that we believe in God because we want to have a happy life, not ask for a lot of things from him and get angry when there is no answer. If we really believe, then God will always be there to give us wisdom and strength."

"You know, ever since I started giving thanks to God like that, my life has always been going up, never down. So God has given me the perception to look at life this way. We will overcome this Multiple Myeloma glitch together just like that. So please don't worry David, God loves you and me. We will win."

I smiled and tried to believe what she said, but it would take a lot more to persuade me. Still, her happy confidence was reassuring.

After the long talks we were both starving, so we never made it to the river. I suggested that we go out to a restaurant to eat. But she insisted that we make dinner at the apartment. Now that she was here with me, I was able to enjoy her excellent Korean cooking.

She cooked a barbecue recipe called L.A. *Kalbi* and we ate it in what is called *sam* style. This consists of sliced beef cooked in a mixture of sesame oil, soy sauce, black pepper, honey, and about twenty sliced garlics. Then you take a leaf of lettuce, add a piece of meat, a teaspoon of rice, and a teaspoon of spicy red sauce called *mak jung*, made from soy bean paste, with chopped mushrooms and green onions. You roll it up and put it into your mouth all together. The taste is fantastic.

Above all, the love that Shin mixed into the meal made me feel warm and comforted.

The Compade medicine that Dr. Portinari prescribed was given as an injection into my blood over a half-hour twice a week. Before they could give me the injection, they needed to take blood, do special blood tests, wait for the results for an hour, and then administer the Compade. So we spent a lot of time over at Dana Farber. Shin selflessly drove me back and forth and sat with me while I gave blood, got medicine, and checked results with Dr. Portinari.

Anyung Haseo, he would say as he entered, proud of his Korean greeting for 'Hello.' He had recently gone on a vacation with his family to Seoul ... and they all loved this fascinating 'miracle' city in Northeast Asia.

We always discussed medical conditions first, but he also took time to chat about life in general and how we were adjusting mentally to the changes. He liked Shin. I think that is true of everyone who meets her.

As I started taking Compade, I had to do another procedure called pheresis to reduce the protein level in my blood. Dr. Portinari explained.

"Basically pheresis is like dialysis. It takes your blood out of one arm, puts it into a machine where it separates the bad plasma from the blood cells and replaces the plasma with another liquid called albumin. Then it pushes the new blood into your other arm. Much cleaner blood after that. You will feel dizzy for about a half-hour but afterwards you will feel wonderful. And it will give the Compade a head start in doing its work."

At first, pheresis was somewhat painful and scary. The needles in each arm were bigger than those for giving or getting blood. Plus the psychological feeling of having all of your blood drained out of your system running across a tube on your stomach is disturbing to think about. I tried listening to music CDs to distract me but that didn't work very well.

The pheresis took about three hours — usually Shin sat patiently by my side and kept me company. During the second pheresis, she had to spend several hours running errands in the city so I was alone with the nurses and the machines.

The red blood flowed out one tube and into the machine. Gushing, analyzing, and processing, a refrigerator-sized contraption takes out what's not supposed to be there. Then it pushes my blood back into my body through another tube exiting the machine with extra drugs to make everything flow smoothly. The smell of hospital alcohol swirls into my nose while literally all of my blood exits and re-enters my body.

The blood pulses across my stomach in a quarter inch clear plastic tube and I hate it. It takes every scrap of mental strength to avoid thinking about what is going on. But each twinge on my chest reminds me sharply and a steady machine hum overwhelms the music I am trying to listen to.

I need so desperately to be with Shin on a beach in the Caribbean and smell the sun tan lotion and play with the vacationers. I long to watch the blue turquoise waves splash on the shore and show Shin the colorful tropical fish in the clear salty water. My bare feet want the sand beneath them and my mouth hungers for the taste of jumbo shrimp with fancy red cocktail sauce and an exotic West Indies drink with rum and pineapples and oranges.

The nurse came by. "Here's your egg salad sandwich and diet coke. How are you feeling?" She left quickly so I didn't have a chance to respond. I felt like I had been churning inside of a cement truck mixer all day. The light vibrations on my stomach didn't hurt at all but it is the worst feeling in the world.

At last Shin returned. She bubbled and smiled and told me about her visits to the stores, who she met, what they looked like, how much the parking cost, what the sunshine was doing. Her voice was lifesaving … I forgot about the machine, the vibrations, the blood. My Shin was entertaining me.

But by the third pheresis the next day, it was getting old and tiresome. Shin closed the magazine she was reading, "I'm boring."

I looked up from a magazine article about China, "What?"

"I'm boring. I have nothing to do."

Suddenly, I was smiling widely for the first time in a month. "Ok, you always want me to correct your English pronunciation and grammar, right?"

"Yes, of course, that's the best way for me to continue my study of English."

"You should say 'I'm bored'. What you said means that people go to sleep when you start talking. A good example is when students talk about certain teachers as boring. That means their lectures are pretty dull."

"So I should say that I'm bored. You know what? I knew that. I just forgot for the moment. Thank you for that, but tell me more."

"Ok, I'll add another word to the grammar lesson. Several times you have told me, 'I'm exciting' when you really mean to say 'I'm excited'. It's the same principle. When you are excited, you are happy, full of energy, about to do fun things. When you say 'I'm exciting,' it means that you are very attractive and interesting and people should want to be around you, especially men. I can say that you're exciting, but you wouldn't usually say that about yourself."

A nurse was in the corner getting supplies out of a cabinet. She burst out laughing, "Oh, sorry, I couldn't help but overhear." "No problem," we all laughed as she left. Happy moments like this made me forget about my deadly cancer and reminded me of wonderful memories of past trips together.

———

Once when I had a business meeting in Milan, I had invited her to come on a driving trip in Italy with me. She was giving me directions from the map. I knew generally that we were heading toward Lake Como — but I couldn't understand why she kept sending me in the wrong direction.

"Are you sure this is the right way?" I asked.

"Without a doubt, of course it is."

The road was too narrow to stop and study the map so I kept driving — she seemed so certain about where are we going. We wandered for a while and eventually found a beautiful small town named Bellagio located on Lake Como. The lakeside scenery there was the most beautiful I have ever seen, although it wasn't exactly the place I had in mind when we started out.

Driving around new places with Shin was always so exiting and fun to me, because she never cared where we were or what the weather was like. Her sense of adventure always inspired me to try new and different things.

She seemed to truly enjoy being lost.

"I love it! Look! Can't you see everything is so different? A first visit is always the best."

Eventually we found a nice little inn with a restaurant and a room with a big double window that opened onto boxes of red flowers overlooking the lake. On the terrace, we had pizza, salad and wine for dinner. The waiter knew some English, so we chatted for a while. He complained that it had been hot and dusty for the last two weeks so it was hard to keep the flowers watered properly.

That night a fantastic thunderstorm finally rolled in with crackling lightening, blowing the curtains, rattling the shutters and chasing away the heat. It was a wonderful catharsis bringing Shin and I closer together, whether we found the right direction or not.

I had a lot of business trips in my career, but with Shin, they were more wonderful then ever before. She was never upset by unexpected difficulties — she always seemed so happy and content. I often tried to absorb her spirit of relaxation when confronting the unknown.

But despite the wonderfully pleasant memories we talked about, I was always glad when the nurse pulled the needles out after pheresis.

———

At first the Compade seemed to be working fine. I was able to go back to work as normal at my office at IEC in Harvard Square. I continued my marketing of telecommunications consulting projects to attorneys and companies who were involved in the newer technologies. These included advanced cell phone services, high speed Internet connections, and using the Internet to substitute for regular telephone service. But although I was an expert in these areas, the success rate in acquiring new clients and projects was going very slowly.

All of the attorneys I met with complimented me on my ideas, but their clients were still not spending much for economic studies yet. This was not expected until next year. In the meantime, my regular mailings, phone calls, and conference speeches continued to establish my reputation. It was a sound investment, but the money coming in was taking a lot longer than I had expected.

I was beginning to get worried about how to pay bills over the next six months.

I had gotten divorced after 25 years of marriage five years ago — right after my youngest daughter, Amy, graduated from college. My wife and I were so different in character, lifestyle, the way we think and what we wanted to do in the future. Right after we married we found that out. But when my son Dan was born three months earlier then a normal baby, it was clear that he needed me. We both loved our children so much, we were determined to stay with them until they were grown up.

So, most of my married life was devoted to my job to support the family and play with my two kids. We spent a lot of time helping Dan make it through school. We helped him study, prepare for tests, and write research papers in high school and college. Amy seemed to do fine on her own, so we encouraged her delightfully independent spirit.

Once in a while, I would think 'Where is my own life? Where is my own happiness?' But the answer was always 'Wait until the kids graduate. Then I will do something different.'

Finally, Dan and Amy were grown up and had finished college, and gotten nice jobs. I had done my task, completed my mission. Even though Dan needs me to visit a lot, as long as I live near him I can do that. 'Finally, I have freedom,' I thought. Out of a sense of responsibility and guilt at the divorce, I had given away almost everything — expensive house, cars, money — to Dan, Amy and my ex-wife.

I figured that with my background and brains, I could always make more money next year. Now all of a sudden, my financial situation was taking a dramatic turn for the worse. And the cancer was destroying any hope of a big consulting year in the near future.

———

I had known Tom Singer, a very senior official in IEC's Harvard Square office, for thirty years, ever since he had been my student at the University of Colorado for a class in statistics. Technically, he was my mentor to review the positive and negative developments in my marketing program and to give advice as to how to proceed. He was a tall athletic guy and in his second year at IEC, he had a reliable client list.

One Thursday, we decided to have lunch to go over our marketing plans. But in the middle of the morning, I started feeling really short of breath and a little dizzy. This was consistent with low hemoglobin, meaning that the bad plasma cells were crowding out the good red blood cells. Which meant that the Compade was probably not working so well since the pheresis should have given me a good head start at the beginning of June. I was getting nervous as I picked him up at his office at noon.

Tom suggested a Thai restaurant, so I readily agreed. I knew there was one across the street so I figured I could make that trip easily. I still had not disclosed my cancer to any colleagues at work outside of the human resources group. I thought that it would impair my image of being able to assist them on their complicated statistical projects, an area where I had a fairly rare and valuable expertise.

As we exited the building, Tom said, "This Thai restaurant is not so good. How about the one across Harvard Square? That has spicier food, nicer tables, and better service."

How could I argue? But it was six blocks away.

Tom set off at a rapid pace, "I'm training for a half-marathon later this summer so any chance for exercise is welcome."

I tried but I couldn't keep up. Tom couldn't help but notice. "By the way, is anything wrong medically? I knew you were in the hospital late last month."

"Nothing serious," I lied. "The doctor noticed something wrong with my blood so he gave me some medicine to take."

But Tom had to keep slowing down to let me catch up. "Is it life-threatening?"

"No. No. The medication should take care of everything. I'll be in good shape in a month."

"Great, you did a terrific job on that other project for us, so we plan to use you again on other consulting assignments."

At the Thai restaurant, I finally got to rest. I was getting a little disoriented and the menu had a hundred entries of bewildering combinations of foods. I quickly ordered one of the specials to save my mental strength to talk about my marketing program. But I could feel something going downhill rapidly inside my body.

Eventually, I got through the meeting. Tom gave some great hints for next steps but overall thought my marketing plan made sense.

"I started out slowly the first year as well. The question will be if there is enough traction with potential clients for the second year."

I assured him that there was. I made an excuse to split up at the restaurant to pick up something at the drugstore. This saved me the double embarrassment of another slow six-block walk back to the office. I sat for a while at a park bench and watched the students head to classes. Back at the office, I checked my email and rested for an hour until Shin picked me up at 4 pm. I was so glad to see her.

———

I collapsed into the passenger seat of the car.

"The meeting with Tom went fine but my internal condition is not good. Extremely short of breath which means low hemoglobin which means Compade is probably not working. I'm a little scared and disappointed."

Shin had asked me not to sugar-coat my medical news as I had done in the past when I was trying to be cheerful and optimistic. Her logic was clear and convincing ... 'As your medical caretaker, I need to have the full facts in order to help you make decisions about how to proceed. Secrets can be disastrous. After all, this is life-threatening cancer.'

I had promised to do as she asked.

She was reassuring, "Just sit back in the seat and close your eyes. I will get you home to rest. In the morning, we will call the doctor if you don't improve. Don't worry about your job right now ... just get some rest. I'm in charge here."

Shin's confidence went far beyond mere words. Her ability to focus on a specific goal and achieve it quickly was phenomenal. When she was in the United States, she had changed her eating habits to include more cheese, shrimp, and a lot of beef. She thought these would help her improve her health combined with her exercise program and playing a lot of golf. However, when she had gone back to Korea to visit her daughters, she went to the doctor for a routine physical.

She had called me from Korea. "Bad news. The doctor complained that my cholesterol level is an unacceptably high 280. I have to reduce this dramatically to get back to normal." So while she was in Korea, she went on her own personal crash 'no-cholesterol' diet, skipping beef, shellfish, eggs, and anything else with bad cholesterol. Forty-five days later, her cholesterol level was 160 ... an amazing transition for the short time period.

"When you want something, you get it," I had told her, "You are amazing."

"I know that," she had answered with a smile. "Many people say 'I'll do it later.' Not me! There is no such sentence in my dictionary. Later? No way. Do it now!"

This single-minded tenacity has always been a source of pride and enjoyment to me as I watched her take on new challenges. Now, for me, it was becoming the very source of my survival. I desperately needed the influence of her stubborn strength of character to conquer this cancer. Now, I literally can not live without her.

Perhaps it was the athletic walk to the Thai restaurant, or perhaps it was just that my time with Compade was coming to a premature end. At any rate, that Thursday night, I crashed.

I had been prone to bleeding slightly from the mouth at nights before May and never paid much attention. I had thought it was a problem with my wisdom teeth. The dentist wanted to take them out, but I had ignored his advice. The bleeding had stopped after I got the new blood at the Pocono Medical Center, so I was thankful for that. But that night the bleeding started and never stopped. I filled up two towels lying on the pillow.

My head ached, I was dizzy, and I couldn't sleep. The next step was clear.

"I think we go see Dr. Portinari first thing in the morning, my darling."

"Yes, he will be able to find another medication to fight the cancer if Compade is not working right now. Don't worry too much David, that was just the first try."

But her voice was full of anxiety and concern. I don't think she slept that night at all. She kept checking to see if I needed another towel for the blood.

As the Compade medicine failed me after only a month, in a towel of blood on my pillow, it reinforced the continuing doubts about my abilities to take care of Shin and give her a wonderful and exciting life. Believe me, incurable cancer can easily sneak in and steal your confidence, no matter where you started out.

Yet I knew deep down in my heart that I had to reverse this depressing attitude, acquire some courage and focus, and do what

I could to move forward. Despite the constant setbacks, I felt that with Shin, we could beat this cancer and re-arrange our lives. But I did not yet have the vision of how this would work.

People always say 'Don't worry about money, at least you have your health.' So what is the new optimistic catch phrase to summarize my predicament? I sure as hell hope there is one. But I haven't heard it yet.

Searching and Adjusting

The bleeding from the mouth had stopped in the morning but we called in to get an appointment with Dr. Portinari anyway. We went to see him at Dana Farber at noon.

"Why are you short of breath?" he asked me in the hall.

"Well, the bleeding all night probably reduced my hemoglobin. No oxygen, no energy."

"I guess so. Let's look at your blood tests and consider a change from Compade. That may not be doing what we want right now. We may be able to use it later in your treatment program. You go and give some blood at the lab. I'll see you in an hour after I look at the test results."

The large waiting room at Dana Farber's main building is more like a nice hotel lobby — filled with current reading materials and comfortable leather furniture. Off to the sides, it opened into suites of rooms to make appointments, give blood, get blood and medicine, an area for consultations with doctors, and an elevator bank to doctors' offices upstairs.

All of the health care providers there are competent, friendly, and encouraging. Off of the lobby, there is even a chapel with a finely carved wooden door that rivaled the churches in Europe.

The gift shop sold the usual candy and books. But they also sold wigs for women undergoing radiation treatments. An excellent cafeteria decorated with Red Sox memorabilia is located one floor down.

After I gave a blood sample for the test, Shin and I looked at the resource library for cancer patients. About half of the material consisted of simplifications of medical terms and procedures, the other half was psychological self-help for cancer patients and families.

"David, with all these books, so many doctors, and such advanced medical facilities, it's hard to believe that they still don't know how to really control Multiple Myeloma yet."

"Good question. I wish I knew the answer."

She seemed so sad when I looked at her, but there was nothing more I could say to cheer her up. She had raised a natural question that was critical to our life together. I couldn't add anything to my response, so I just held her hand tightly.

Luckily, with the efficiency of the lab, it only took 45 minutes to get the results into the computer. The nurse came out to the lobby to get us. Shin was apprehensive as we headed to the doctor consultation area. But I was starting to feel upbeat — I knew I was in the right place.

The nurse recorded my weight, temperature, and blood pressure and then directed me to a small consultation room to wait for the doctor. It had several chairs, a computer terminal, and an examining table.

Dr. Portinari had his usual optimistic attitude.

"Ok, I've looked at the results and we are going to do three things. First, let's get several units of blood into you tomorrow. Second, a couple more pheresis treatments to clean your blood up again. Third, let's switch off of Compade onto another option that I mentioned before — a combination of Thalidomide and Dexamethasone, a treatment we call 'Thal-Dex' for short. That could have 80% effectiveness in your situation."

"I remember you discussing that earlier. It sounds fine to me. What's involved? "

"Remember the Thalidomide babies from the 1950's who were deformed at birth?"

"Sure, that was a big deal with a drug not fully tested when I was a kid. From what I remember, the pills were given to pregnant mothers in Europe because it was thought to prevent nausea. However, several years later many babies were born with arms and legs undeveloped because the drug had prevented blood from reaching those areas in the womb."

"Right. Now we have found that it has a very beneficial impact in the fight against Multiple Myeloma cancer. Because the drug prevents blood from reaching the cancerous cells, it slows down the spread of cancer in your blood. The results are even better when combined with Dexamethasone, a steroid that intensifies the impact in your system. This steroid is totally different from the ones that some athletes have taken. So you won't get a lot of new muscles."

He smiled.

This sounded pretty good to me. But I wondered, do I really have a choice here?

"What are the side effects?" I asked.

"The problem is that you don't take the steroids every day. During the month, some weeks are on and some are off. When you are not taking steroids, you may get some physical and mental symptoms that are unpleasant. These include sleeplessness, fatigue, mild depression, swelling of the face and stomach, and possibly shaky hands. Keep me up to date on the side effects as I measure how effective Thal-Dex is at reducing the bad cancer-related proteins in your blood."

"How about the bleeding from last night?"

"The new blood tomorrow and the pheresis will take care of that. Just relax tonight."

"Ok," I said, "Thanks for the quick response." I was starting to worry about the new list of possible side effects but I guess anything was better than blood flowing from your mouth all night.

We were hungry and tired, so Shin and I left for the apartment as Dr. Portinari hurried off to another appointment. While we drove back to Cambridge, I pondered my fate. I had only lasted one month on the first treatment choice. When we had first discussed it, it was a miracle drug and I had high hopes for a quick effect. Now I'm out of the Compade clinical trial program and on to something else. Not a great track record for me so far. But I kept a positive attitude.

On Saturday while I was getting blood, I joked with the Compade nurses that I had been 'kicked out of the program'. They were trained to be supportive and positive so they smiled and politely asked about the next steps. But I don't think they got the joke. I'm not sure even why I said it that way. Actually it wasn't really very funny anyway.

———

But many days, the truly depressing setbacks just didn't seem to register. Work seemed to be under control, there was still weekend time for road trips that Shin loved, and we were on to the next medical treatment that had a good track record.

While we drove around rural New England, Shin taught me various words and phrases in Korean as well as Korean history, customs, and the culture difference between Korea and the United States.

And she was a wonderful storyteller.

"Once when I lived in Seoul, I learned a real lesson about the difference between Korean and American breakfasts. You remember my friend John, right?"

"Sure, he was a college graduate student who taught English in a high school in Korea."

"That's right. Years ago, he got married to a Korean girl who had a pharmacy in Kyungju which is about four hours from Seoul. One time, his father came from the United States to visit them. I picked him up at the airport and he stayed at my house in

Seoul overnight, before heading off to see his son and daughter-in-law the next morning."

She smiled to herself, remembering back.

"This was his first time in Korea and I wanted to treat him like a very special guest. Plus I wanted to show him many of our Korean foods while he stayed in Seoul. We had to leave early in the morning so I got up at 4:30 to prepare a big breakfast for him. I cooked the most wonderful Korean traditional meal. By 5:30 when he woke up, I had a table full of great things --- spicy fermented cabbage called *kimchi,* pancakes with green onions and clams called *pa jun,* noodles with pork and vegetables called *chopje,* dried spicy anchovies with honey called *mielchi bokum,* and soup called *dwenjun gigae.* Most Koreans eat this bubbling hot soup every morning. It is similar to the Japanese-style *miso* but with a slightly different taste. It also has mushrooms, onions, and a little beef. And of course a nice bowl of rice."

I smiled widely, imagining the look on his face when he saw what he had to eat.

"Do you have some milk?" he asked tentatively.

Shin recoiled acting out the scene as if it were yesterday.

"Sure, I said to him as I brought it to the table."

Then quietly, "Do you have some sugar?"

"I will find some."

"He proceeded to mix the milk and sugar with the rice and quickly eat the whole bowl. After that, he left the table and said that we better hurry to meet his son on time. I was in shock. I couldn't believe it … Except for the rice, he didn't even touch a thing."

She leaned back, marveling at the naiveté of her youth.

"Even though I had been to the United States once before, I had no idea what a traditional American breakfast was. I was so surprised when I finally learned the difference. And even though

I have been here dozens of time since then, I still have a hard time eating cold breakfast cereal with sugar like you do."

I tickled her playfully.

"I'm sure you notice that I never ever eat dried anchovies for breakfast ... even though I do like honey."

Since I love languages and anything about Korea, listening to her stories always made me happy — I quickly forgot about my troubles.

Plus, I had gotten word that the health insurance was paying for everything despite the earlier confusion. It was easy to slip into a dream world atmosphere.

———

After the initial setback, things settled into a fairly normal pattern. I took the Thal-Dex pills on a prescribed schedule and saw Dr. Portinari once a month. My health condition seemed to stabilize and Shin started me on a diet.

She said "You really need to lose weight! It's for your health."

She was playful but serious.

"How about if we eat small portions, and much more vegetables such as yams, asparagus, broccoli, garlic, tomatoes and mushrooms? And also different kinds of nuts and beans. When we eat meat, I will make sure it has very little fat."

"Sounds good to me."

I had always wanted to lose some weight so I was grateful for her dedication. I had never had anyone take care of me so effectively.

We also joined the local health club across from my office. So while Shin exercised and used the sauna, I swam in the pool. Dr. Portinari had recommended moderate exercise so this was a big help.

Summer weather was pleasant, sailboats floated on the Charles River, and classical music concerts were frequent. We also spent time exploring the New England coastline from New Hampshire to Cape Cod to Rhode Island. Day by day, our activities seemed to give me more and more physical and emotional strength.

Shin had found a delightful 'Par 3' golf course in Lexington that we started playing at. She would wear nice white pants, a shirt with drawings of dogs on it, golf shoes, small white gloves, and a pink visor from Korea advertising cosmetics. Her smile was truly beautiful in the delightful summer sun. And she seemed so happy to be getting me to do exercise outdoors.

The Par 3 idea is that each hole is like a regular golf course but limited to anywhere between 30 and 150 yards. So there were bridges over a small river, sand traps, rough areas, and trees curving onto the course. For me, it was a wonderful shortcut to the golfing experience without a lot of practice. Since my only golf knowledge was limited to TV watching and miniature golf, I was pretty pathetic. But since the other players around the course were generally not experts, I did not feel embarrassed when it took me 6 shots to do a Par 3 hole.

However, Shin was an excellent teacher and gave me great confidence. By focusing on just 35 yd and 85 yard shots and not panicking on the putts, I was able to finish respectably.

"I'm very optimistic today. How about a $10 bet for the lowest score?" I smiled.

"You definitely have started kicking this cancer. I can feel the medicine working just by looking at your face. No evidence of mild depression here. Ok it's a deal — $10 to the winner."

The amazing result that day was a tie. I think she intentionally held back to make me feel good. Anyway it was good fun and it gave me a needed boost.

———

Since the medicine was working out fine with minimal side effects, I was able to work often at my office in Harvard Square. Shin frequently went to local nine-hole golf courses in the area, got exercise, and met new people. That made me feel good because she had taken lessons in Korea and was a pretty decent golfer, and that was the least I could do for her.

Later that week I took her to the Gardner museum in Boston and a special dinner at the top of the Prudential Center nearby. The museum is in a sixteenth century Italian palace reconstruction in the middle of Boston and contains fabulous paintings from the Italian Renaissance.

I felt a special pleasure showing Shin some of the things that I knew about Europe. Her Korean experience had mixed with American vistas to produce a view that had no architecture that was 500 years old.

"Look at what they were doing back then," she exclaimed. I had to remind myself that South Korea, despite a history of thousands of years, has been totally rebuilt since the war in the early 1950's, so most of the buildings there are more modern than here. I felt honored and pleased to be able to show her what I knew about Western Europe.

I had picked the restaurant because of its excellent location on the 52nd floor of the Prudential Center. The white tablecloths, crystal, and silver combined with the glass and shiny metal of the restaurant's architecture. The windows provided magnificent views of the setting sun in the summer sky.

As we walked around the top floor on that clear August evening, we could see for miles in all directions. Hope was bubbling over as Shin marveled at all the places to go and things to do.

"There's MIT, there's the Museum of Fine Arts, there's Copley Square for shopping, there's Boston harbor with the boats. Oh, there's Logan Airport with the planes landing and taking off to far-off places. There is so so much to do with you David. I love this place. I love you."

"I love you too my dearest precious darling. I brought you here tonight to thank you for how much you've done for me."

She smiled with content, "It is so much fun to be with you."

"We will see all these places together Shin, I guarantee."

But every time these words come out of my mouth, an alarm clock goes off in my brain and the doubts wake me up. Cancer is a thief. Don't ever forget that. I wonder if that is a good excuse for un-kept promises.

Even though the effects of my cancer seemed to be less overt and oppressive, I started to notice subtle changes in my attitudes toward people and situations. After all, I still had an incurable cancer — a lot of optimism but not really the greatest prognosis for long term survival.

One odd situation that always used to annoy me was poor retail store designs. For example, it was impossible to go to the prescription desk on the second floor of the Harvard Square CVS without cutting right through the middle of a line of people waiting to pay for purchases on the first floor. It was as if the store architects had intentionally constructed the store so that the customer line would block access to the pharmacy area upstairs. I used to think 'Why couldn't they change this? It is so obvious what's going on.'

A similar kind of problem existed at various fast food stores like Dunkin Donuts. Many times you order from one person who prepares the food and drinks and then you pay another person at the cash register. In a lot of cases, you have to repeat your whole order to the cash register person even though they are two feet from the person you just spoke to. Why couldn't you just order once?

Anyway, small things, but they used to annoy me. Now, however, a new mind-set was taking hold of my brain. Especially in my condition, these were clearly not things that mattered in the grand scheme. If my mind was to be occupied, this was not the right stuff to be putting there.

I tried to relax a little and take daily life a little bit more like it was presented to me. 'What's the big hurry anyway?' I would tell myself, 'Take a long, deep breath and enjoy the oxygen.'

Yet there were always times when I could not shake a more sober view of my predicament. On one day in particular, I felt like a three hundred pound weight had been placed on my chest — sort of like the symptoms of a heart attack.

It was gray and rainy and cool. Sitting in the bookstore coffee shop by the window, I was reading and typing and watching the people go by. I always used to like this position. The changing action seemed to be a pleasant background to my work. All of a sudden, though, it became incredibly depressing. Virtually every single person going by, no matter what their status or looks or wealth, will live longer than me.

A girl walked by smiling to herself about some pleasant memory or plan. A woman had two kids and some packages from the grocery store. A retired guy wearing a Red Sox sweatshirt wandered by, still aglow from a recent win. The wind brought in a light drizzle. The people I had been watching seemed unconcerned about the rain. They all had plans for later that day — and later in life.

'Wake up, you're dying soon,' I said to myself. For me, all of the media talk about beating some of the more popular cancers was a misleading distraction. Of course, I was happy for the success and public recognition of the need to mount multiple efforts to slow down this medical tornado. 'Cancer Survivor' sounded like a really great status symbol for those with the mental and physical strength to come out winners.

But it didn't really apply to Multiple Myeloma — especially at my advanced stage. It's not even very localized … this stuff is in the bloodstream and the bone marrow. It's everywhere. Even in the best case, we are just extending my life several years with drugs that are bound to have life-changing side effects. 'Wake up,' I told myself.

I took my glasses off and wiped my eyes. Ok, maybe I should avoid the window from now on.

I also began to miss the past successes of my professional career. Why couldn't I take a moment of time from my past and just go back there now? Not start over, but just freeze time back when things were going great.

I had been an internationally known expert on the economics of the telephone industry. I had appeared on TV, radio, in all the major newspapers. Most of the time, I had provided solid insight into developments in the rapidly changing technology of the Internet. I was a frequent speaker at conferences and reporters filled my voicemail with requests for interviews.

I had worked for a large global consulting company and served as an expert advisor to some of the largest communications companies in the world. My email was always full of requests for help on current projects. I had made several accurate forecasts and my name carried an aura of respect among those who tracked the industry. I traveled a lot and felt at home in airports and restaurants. Career-wise, I had done pretty well with a Ph.D. in Economics. The work was interesting and challenging.

Now with cancer, it was all fading away quickly. The things that I had accomplished seemed to have happened a long time ago. There was no uncertainty about where I was on my career path. There were no decisions to be made … I had no control. I felt like I was on a ski slope that had no end. No skis, just sitting down — sliding and sliding.

It wasn't a case of taking a break from success and then returning to my former fame. I was done. It was over. Signing off, good-by, good-night. I miss the bright lights but no one is offering me a choice anymore. I began to wonder 'How much time is safe to spend on memories of the past without going crazy?'

But despite my desire to transport myself back in time, I always envisioned Shin right there at my side. After several years of chasing her, and longing for her, I finally have her. Just when I desperately need her mental strength and inner power to deal with my awful situation.

Maybe she was right — God sent her to me to be my best and only friend while I am here on this earth. Now she is sharing everything with me, the serious and the silly, the work and the play, the happy and the sad. It was impossible to visualize my life without her.

In August, we had great news from Shin's oldest daughter, Ejin, who had graduated several years ago. She had met a psychiatrist and was going to get married. We celebrated happily ... this would make it easier for Shin to spend more time with me.

She felt that it is important for Ejin and Ehang to get married before she could be totally free. Somehow, the social status of re-married mothers is not great in Korea, despite its ready acceptance in the United States. So I have been waiting patiently out of a sense of duty to her girls.

Shin was ecstatic about the upcoming wedding.

"I am so so happy. Her fiancé sounds like just the right husband to take care of my daughter. Now I can let go of her. She can be my best friend and we will wait for the younger daughter to find her husband at the bank where she works."

"That is fantastic news Shin! I have never seen you so excited. I am so happy for you."

"So David, I have to go to Korea to arrange the wedding for two months. I should leave at the end of August. Will you be Ok with that?"

"Absolutely! With my cancer medications going fine, I can take care of myself. Just give me reports every week. I have waited twenty years to meet you, and chased you for such a long time, and now I've finally almost captured you. You are the light and hope and strength of my life. I'll wait patiently."

"I'll be back after the wedding and we will be smiling, talking, and playing very soon."

I couldn't resist some optimism, "Everything is going according to our plan."

In reality, it hurt so bad to say those words, and to just let her go like this for two months, but I had no choice … plus, she had earned it.

Soon after that, it was time for her to leave for Korea. The day dawned rainy, cloudy, and cool as it sometimes does in late summer along the coast. We hadn't slept much. Shin had packed the night before … she is always so efficient, it only takes five minutes. Most of the suitcase was full of wedding gifts for her daughter. And for friends and relatives, she brought an assortment of vitamins like Centrum Silver that seemed hard to get in Korea.

The airport terminal in Boston was almost empty at 5 am. The early morning flight stopped at San Francisco and then continued on to Seoul later that day. She never likes long drawn out goodbyes, so she asked me to go back to the apartment and go back to sleep. But I insisted that we sit and snuggle for a half-hour while we woke up and waited for her flight time.

Shin was wearing comfortable black silk pants and a turquoise blue top with sequins. She tended to dress up for airplane flights because she would see many other Koreans on the plane and that was their style. She even wore a slight amount of makeup on her face which she usually did not do for me since I preferred the natural look.

We carved out a warm spot on some comfortable benches by United's domestic terminal to rest and say goodbye. I felt that we were sitting at a campfire under the stars in the California desert. Hot flickering bits of light floated skyward while the bright heat of the fire warmed our hearts and made all our dreams so possible. Hope and excitement sprayed from the stars dotting the dark black sky.

Others nearby talked in hushed tones recognizing the sanctity of the event. The pungent smell of burning hickory brought forth a lifetime of fond camping memories.

Suddenly, it seemed that I was all alone and almost abandoned in the middle of nowhere, worried that I would never see her again. To myself, I thought, 'Shin, you must come back! Please, come back to me like you said. Promise that you will return one more time. Then, I'll never let you go anywhere without me, please don't leave me here alone.'

Although my mind was thinking these anxious words, instead, I said weakly,

"Have a great trip — don't worry about me — give my best to your daughters. Congratulations on Ejin's wedding, and have a wonderful time in Korea."

My stomach was tied in knots as we kissed good-bye. Her beautiful face was wet with tears … hiding the same desperately miserable feeling that I had … 'Why did we have to be apart, why, why, why?' Her warm hand in mine, it seemed we could never let go.

And then she was gone.

I sat back in the chair exhausted. The airport used to be quite exciting, the beginning of a new adventure. But this morning I was in a desert without even a bottle of water.

I can't remember ever really crying much over fifty odd years. Perhaps everything had gone too well in my life. Perhaps my character was too optimistic, too constructive for that kind of sentimental outpouring. Possibly I blocked out memories of things that might grab my heart.

But driving back to the apartment, the tears would not stop. This was no ordinary parting. Although we would be back together in a couple of months, my brain would have to deal all alone with my rapidly declining health. And the Thal-Dex medication did cause periodic depression and physical side effects like shaky hands, fatigue, lack of focus, and a puffy face.

I had no friends and relatives to talk with — no support group, no casual acquaintances to go to the movies with, or church members to eat dinner with. This had all been by choice, of course, so I was not bitter and had no regrets. It was just a fact of life. But it was a weakness that cancer could easily exploit.

———————

Back at the apartment in Harvard Square, I felt as if all my strength was gone, disappearing with Shin as she flew halfway across the world. It was impossible to work and I had no important meetings. So I decided to avoid the office that day and watch a movie at home.

I picked a Korean DVD that Shin had bought in Korea last year to help me learn Korean language conversation. It was called 'Christmas in August.' She had never seen the movie, but the clerk at the store had recommended it. I had not yet seen it, but it had English subtitles so it should be easy to follow.

It was the story of a middle-aged guy who owned a photography store in Seoul and a younger girl who worked for the traffic department giving tickets to illegally parked cars. He spent his time sitting in his shop at the window watching her work on the street for hours and hours.

Then, a cute, almost romantic, relationship develops between the two. They ride a motorbike smiling in the rain and sometimes even kiss a little. Periodically, he disappears to the doctor's office for tests of some kind. But he always pretended as if nothing was wrong.

At the end of the movie, when they started to fall in love with each other, he writes a letter to the girl and puts her photo in the store window. Then he dies of cancer.

I just did not see this coming. Why does this meanness sneak up on me like that? Can't it wait until I'm a little stronger?

The Bankruptcy Attorney

At the airport before she left, Shin held my hand and whispered, "While I'm not here, don't mope around, work hard, take care of your body, keep checking your weight and eat good decent food. Then when I come back, I'll continue to take care of you, and we can have a lot of playtime together too. Ok?"

But after a couple of days, I started to miss her a lot. Her bright smile and happy voice were now an essential part of my life — like a sky full of bright stars on a dark night. The way she took care of me had the touch of a delightful partner combined with the strength of a loving mother. She did call me from Korea almost every morning to check to see what I was eating and doing. But that didn't seem to cheer me up.

I tried to keep busy to cure my loneliness. So far, the chemotherapy drugs seemed to be controlling the cancer cells without creating pronounced side effects in my body. I worked at the office every day, then took a swim at the health club, then ate at a restaurant and headed home to watch TV and go to bed.

But after several weeks, I began to notice some serious side effects of the chemotherapy medications. One day, I woke up and could not type on the computer. My hands were shaking so much that it was impossible to answer email or work on an article discussing the future of the Internet that I had wanted to finish that day. My heart seemed to be beating twice as fast as normal. I felt exhausted even though I had slept all night. I guess I knew that my body might react to the drugs in these ways. Perhaps Shin's presence here had postponed the symptoms. But now, my loneliness seemed to enhance the effects,

63

The major culprit was likely the steroids. The Dexamethasone that I was taking had a complicated schedule of off-
days and on-days. These were designed to help reduce the cancer effects in my blood and control the symptoms of Multiple
Myeloma. Unfortunately, with the on-again, off-again schedule,
my body and brain had to adjust to 'steroid withdrawal' several
times a month. Dr. Portinari had mentioned that I might feel
slightly depressed during withdrawal, but today was bringing a
lot of physical effects that I had not expected.

I felt the pressure building inside of me. I really needed to
finish my article and spend some time at the office. But I felt so
bad, I couldn't concentrate and I looked terrible. I decided to
avoid an appearance at work.

Instead, I took a long walk towards Harvard University to
collect my thoughts and try to get some fresh air to clear my head.
The streets were crowded with students going to and from class.
I passed by Sanders Hall, a hundred-year old stone and brick
church building which now housed a large cafeteria and a small
concert auditorium. I passed Baxter Library and Harvard's world
renowned Fogg Art Museum. After several years living in the
apartment, I had not been to either one yet, but it seemed comforting to have them nearby.

I reached Harvard Yard where students, teachers, and tourists
were relaxing and studying in the grass-covered courtyard surrounded by classrooms and dormitories. Walking out of the
Yard toward the stores and restaurants, I came to the big intersec-
tion with the news stands. The street seemed to be a maze of
cars, trucks, and busses.

All of a sudden, I felt light-headed and dizzy. Students on
bicycles appeared from out of nowhere. My legs seemed to
weaken. I reached out to hold onto a lamppost to steady myself.
I was shocked and disappointed to find out that I couldn't get
across the street.

Figuring that I would be better safe than sorry, I turned back to the protection of the courtyard. My body was sweating and shaking. I had panicked trying to get across the street. Was a smart brain warning me about new physical limitations? Or was my mental condition so screwed up that it was fabricating an imaginary world of potential dangers? In either case, this was not a good sign.

I recovered enough to understand that I should assess how bad things were really getting. I decided to use my cell phone to check my voicemail at work. Yet my hands were shaking so much that I could not dial the number. Even my fingers could not navigate the menu to get the right entry out of the phonebook in its memory. After several tries, I gave up. I still had enough logic left to realize not to frustrate myself so much that I make things even worse.

In order to catch my breath, I sat on the steps of a classroom building next to a statue that was popular with visitors. Apparently, it had been highlighted in the guidebooks and everyone needed a photo of themselves there. So there was a steady stream of happy tourists to watch. But nobody paid any attention to me and my loneliness. The contrast made me feel even worse.

Time passed and nothing happened. I didn't get better. I didn't get worse. Just nothing. I seemed almost paralyzed ... unable to move. That made me nervous. My body seemed out of control. And my brain did not understand. But I did know that it was not the cancer talking, it was the side effects of the medications to control it.

As the sun set, I got cold.

'Am I dying like this?' I thought.

People headed home from work and classes ... lights went on in the dormitory rooms. I got colder sitting on the stone steps. Finally, I summoned the strength to stand up and travel the five blocks back to my apartment. My walk was slow and unsteady but I finally made it.

———————

The three-story red brick apartment building was typical of those on Kirkland Street in Cambridge. There are six units in the building and I lived on the second floor on the right. I have a large map of Western Europe on one wall and numerous framed photos of Shin throughout the big room that doubles as a living and dining area. Another wall featured a map of the world with China in the center.

A wooden table covered with green tiles holds my laptop computer connected to the Internet. Several bookcases were filled with books on computer technology, mathematics, economics, and European languages. One shelf was filled with music CDs by Bach, Beethoven, Brahms, Mozart, Vivaldi, and Chopin. While familiar, the apartment seemed strange and foreign, like a movie you can't remember if you've seen or not.

I was used to living alone, and it had never bothered me before. But now I felt completely lonely and empty. I missed Shin desperately.

I walked through the small kitchen area into the bedroom.

The double bed made me smile. Before Shin had gone to Korea, she bought new sheets and blankets and pillows to keep me company. One quilt was a pale yellow with red roses and on top of that another burgundy cover with dark red flowers on a pattern of stripes. The pillowcases were dark blue with bunches of pink and white flowers with green leaves. She told me the dark colors would disguise the stains if I had another bleeding episode. When the sun came through the windows in the mornings, the bed was radiant, smiling, and comfortable.

A wooden dresser held my small collection of clothes that Shin had lovingly folded and organized for me. On top of the dresser were a dozen containers with my anti-cancer medications. The Thal-Dex of course, but also two antibiotics, something to prevent stomach irritation, and six different vitamins to replace things in my blood that the other medicines tended to deplete.

The calcium-vitamin D pills were particularly important in my case. One of the eventual problems with my cancer was that it weakened the bones leaving the possibility of easy fractures. In later stages, actual bumps begin to appear on them — something that others said can be quite painful.

So the calcium was a big deal to strengthen the bones while the other medications were fighting the cancer in my blood. I hope this pain never comes. I have never been able to deal with it very well.

Shin had stocked the refrigerator and cabinets with things to prepare quickly. Japanese Udong soup, Korean style vegetable dumplings called *mandu*, rice, packages of mushrooms and fresh vegetables, and a variety of juices. It was as if she had tried to create an aura to protect me from harm while she was away.

Unfortunately, the stress of the new limitations that I was finding out actually made me scared so I wasn't very hungry. But somewhere in my logic was the idea that if I didn't eat, I would make things much worse. I ate a bowl of Udong soup with red pepper powder on it and drank a glass of orange juice.

I fell asleep on the couch after fifteen minutes.

Later that night, I woke up briefly and took my medicine. I tried to go back to sleep but I couldn't. I looked at my collection of movies — 'Apollo 13', 'Top Gun', 'Chocolat', and 'Amadeus', where the heroes face challenges and uncertainty with courage and determination. I settled on 'Out of Africa', which I had always tried to imitate for its sense of adventure into the unknown. No doubt that spirit helped me find Shin.

Eventually, I stumbled to the bedroom where I collapsed on the bed trying to erase the day's events from my memory.

———

It was certainly true that I had experienced side effects when Shin was here as well. Several times, the mood swings leading to judgment errors and erratic behavior caught me by surprise. Over my lifetime, I have had a pretty steady positive outlook and didn't go to extremes — never dwelling on negative outlooks or past mistakes that I had made. And my discussions with others were almost always diplomatic. I was never harsh or critical.

But one day, the medicine caught up with me and I made a serious mistake when talking with Shin. The medication descriptions had warned about possible lapses in judgment, but I had figured that it wouldn't happen to me. But it did. And it was not good.

Shin frequently talked to other patients at Dana Farber as she was waiting for me to get or give blood or get medication. On occasion, she would run into someone who had Multiple Myeloma and had survived five years or even more. Some had even gone into remission — meaning that the cancer seemed to go away for a while, perhaps for years at a time.

One day when she was describing the positive outlook, she said, "David, I met three people who have the same cancer that you have. Several have been alive for five years, and one has made it for almost ten years!"

"Shin, there is an interesting statistical difficulty with the optimistic assessment there. Many people don't realize it fully. It's called the 'sample selection problem'."

I had studied lots of complicated statistics with the economics so I was pretty familiar with a particular problem that applied to her conclusion. I had even taught graduate students about it so I was pretty comfortable that I knew what I was talking about.

"Suppose ten people have Multiple Myeloma. We hear about two people who live five years with a series of expert medical treatments. And one who has lived ten years. The naïve conclusion is that we are in the same boat. Celebrate! We've got at least five years. The big problem is that the three people we're basing our conclusion on is a 'selected sample.' Unfortunately, we can't interview the other seven … they're dead."

I said the word 'dead' in a humorous way but it didn't help. I wished I could take back my words as soon as I had spoken.

She was crestfallen. Maybe it hadn't occurred to her in just that way. Most likely it was the sharp and factual way that I said it. Her lips curled and quivered with a deep and silent hurt that only her mouth could show. She turned away, perhaps to hide a tear, perhaps to bite her lip.

"Oh," she whispered so quietly.

"I'm so so sorry. I didn't mean to tell you that. I was trying to show off my statistical expertise. I don't think that applies to us anyway."

"David, with confidence and God's wisdom, what's not possible?" Her soft voice was trying so hard to dismiss my stupid observation.

But the damage was done. My frustration had hurt her even if I was being accurate. This was not good at all. She was my angel, my hope and light, the only person I really needed. 'What an idiot I was!' I told myself. I would never ever do such a mean thing again. Later, I cried when I was alone. Why had I hurt her? But was it really my fault?

'Come on,' I told myself, 'don't make excuses. Don't do it again. Period.' I don't want to be mean. Even if I am dying of cancer. I became determined to never ever make that mistake again.

———————

The next day, I was able to make it into the office. The long sleep seemed to have eased the side effects that I had been experiencing. I felt relieved. Maybe it was just a one-time occurrence. I checked the calendar and saw that my next meeting with the doctor was the following week, so I figured that I would be fine until then. I would take it easy and do some reading that I had put off for the last several months.

My office had a nice view of the courtyard next to the Charles Hotel near Harvard Square. It was large even for management consulting executives. I had a big desk and a separate table and chairs for private meetings. Shin had helped me bring in over a thousand textbooks that I had accumulated over the years. The five bookcases gave the image of real scholarship. Of course, I had not read all of them. But I knew where to go when the relevant issue came up. It was essentially my own personal research library.

The manager of the Harvard Square office, John Millard, was a slim, intense economist with a nervous appearance. An expert in the energy industry, he had worked many years in Alaska and now spent a lot of time herding the diverging interests in the office. He also dealt with headquarters on financial matters.

Later that day, while they were doing the budget for next year, John walked into my office. I had been relaxing and reading a recent research report about the Internet.

"We found a huge error in the computer that affected your payroll. We've been overpaying you by a substantial amount for the last ten months."

"What? I noticed the change when I was promoted to Managing Director. I assumed the new salary went with the promotion."

"No, No. That was just a clerical error in the computer. The treasurer at headquarters will reduce the salary back to the original amount beginning the next pay period."

I was in shock. My office, although quite large, started closing in on me.

"I don't know why no one here or at headquarters ever caught this. But the treasurer wants a check for the amount that was overpaid so far this year."

"Look, the marketing program is going quite well and we should have plenty of projects early next year. Why don't we wait for the discrepancy to clear itself up as you pay me for the new client work?"

"The treasurer doesn't want to wait. He is not giving me a choice here."

"But I don't have that kind of money sitting around."

"In that case, he suggested that you sign a promissory note where we deduct something each month from the revised salary check until the overpayment is paid back. Headquarters is not giving me any leeway on this."

He seemed to be following the company line without much analysis or reaction to a fairly massive and long term 'clerical error' as he called it.

"Well, have headquarters email me a draft of the note and let me think about it for a couple of days."

He left my office abruptly, not knowing what else to say.

What should I do now? What could I do? One disaster after another. I was demoralized.

My options were limited. My guess was that if I disputed their decision, my automatic salary deposit every two weeks would stop immediately until we resolved the issue. That would be a real financial disaster. And what about my health insurance? An attorney to contest the issue would likely have the same impact. It was looking like I would have to sign the promissory note and agree to the monthly payments. At least then my health insurance would be safe.

But there was a huge and immediate problem. My salary was now cut in half. With the reduced paycheck, I could not pay my bills … not even close.

For most of my adult life I had not worried about money that much. But at this moment, my financial security seemed to disappear overnight. Another part of my life was spinning out of control … not life threatening like cancer, but still a major catastrophe.

I quickly made an appointment with a Cambridge bankruptcy attorney who I found in the Yellow Pages. He had time on Monday. I knew that it would be embarrassing, upsetting some people, but I had to move quickly now.

To make matters worse, it was becoming clear that I couldn't really continue my professional consulting career very much longer. People at work had started to notice my deteriorating physical appearance.

At my office at IEC, I had been helping Tom and a colleague with a complicated business strategy decision that required calculations and insights that I had developed to guide large communications companies. Although my advice was world class, Tom noticed my poor appearance and unsteady walk.

"How's the health?"

"Oh fine," I lied. "Shin is away in Korea so I have been eating too much fast food. That must have caused the weight gain. She'll be back soon, get me on a regular Korean food diet, and I'll look much better in a month."

"Actually I have a book that talks about 'Sharpening the Saw'. Let me loan it to you. That chapter stresses how important physical exercise is in the overall profile of successful people. I just ran a half-marathon and it seems like my work has taken a turn for the better."

"Sure, that's great, I'll take a look."

It was still too early to tell work colleagues about cancer. But the handwriting was on the wall. The decline in my physical condition was a disappointing contrast with a previous fifty-four years essentially free of health problems.

Now, I knew that the professional consulting career would disappear quickly with the obvious appearance of medical problems — even for those who don't know the cancer details. Colleagues at the office might show a little sympathy, but for potential clients, it was a rotten marketing image.

The side effects grew more pronounced. Some days, when I looked in the mirror, I was shocked to see the person there. A red puffy face from the steroids made me almost unrecognizable. A bloated stomach exaggerated my overweight condition.

I pulled out the file of literature that Dr. Portinari had provided about the Thal-Dex medications. We hadn't discussed side effects very much but now the printed warnings opened my eyes to a more depressing and frightening outlook.

There it was in black and white. Possible side effects included shaky hands, lightheadedness, tingling in the feet and fingers, increased heart rate, disorientation, puffy face and stomach, body aches, sleeplessness, mild depression, cramps in the hands and calves, and increased risk of infections.

I had always thought the side effects were associated with the steroids that I was taking. Now I found that Thalidomide too was creating the problems in my system.

One item scared me to death.

'Patients should watch for uneven swelling in the legs and elsewhere which may indicate evidence of blood clots which could cause a heart attack.'

What? Not only was I dying of cancer with several years to go, but now I had to worry about a sudden heart attack crushing my chest and robbing me of the little time I had left.

Where was fairness?

Where was balance?

Where the hell was hope?

Over the weekend, I prepared for my meeting with the bankruptcy attorney on Monday. Back five years ago, my financial situation had been pretty good. Salary was excellent and money was saved for retirement in IRA accounts.

But the divorce was a big financial drain. That was an intentional choice. On top of that, though, the bursting of the Internet and telecom bubble on the West Coast had cut into my expected income.

I withdrew all my money from the Individual Retirement Accounts and used that to live on. This was supplemented with credit cards. Under normal circumstances, I felt that my career would always head up again and the salary would increase to previous levels. Then I would be able to recover and pay back debts and save for the future. Before cancer, that used to be the plan. Now, unfortunately, normal times had left me … most likely forever.

Several weeks earlier, I had received notices from the Internal Revenue Service and the Massachusetts Department of Revenue. It turns out that I owed a lot of money in taxes because I had prematurely withdrawn money from the IRA accounts. Thus, despite all the government talk about helping the unemployed, they were doing everything they could to strip me of what meager savings I had left and help force me into a financial disaster.

The internal stress started to build. My heart was beating twice as fast, I would sweat everywhere I went, and I had to hold the hand railing going up and down stairs. Stress had joined the cancer in my blood — now I had two poisons attacking me.

My brain was trying to sort out dozens of options. I knew that bankruptcy would go on my credit report and wasn't sure how that would affect my ability to earn money in the future.

With no credit cards, how would I buy airplane tickets or make hotel reservations?

I prepared a one page summary of my debts and monthly bills and compared it with my new lower salary. Expenses were double my income. There was no way to make it work out. After a quick stop at the office in the morning, I went over to the attorney's office at two in the afternoon. My hands were shaking as I drove into the parking lot near his office.

The stately colonial red brick buildings in Bullfinch Square across from the Cambridge courthouse housed a series of attorneys' offices. In the center of the buildings was a courtyard with a flower garden, landscaped trees, park benches and a gazebo.

Most of the attorneys that hurried by had expensive dark suits and nice silk ties. I used to dress like that once. But that was before ... when I was important and successful, I thought.

Arnie Burley was a young, energetic attorney who had learned the bankruptcy procedures from his father. The conference room had a large wooden table, nice leather chairs and was surrounded by bookcases of law books. In the corner was a grandfather clock next to photos of the firm's founders on the wall. A large floor to ceiling window opened onto the courtyard.

I was sweating as he studied the personal financial information that I had put together. With the 50% reduction in the IEC salary, my existing debts, and the new promissory note, I couldn't pay my bills ... especially the credit cards.

He leaned back on the rear two legs of his chair against the wall and played with a pen.

"You're perfect for Chapter 7 bankruptcy ... liquidation. Wipe out your credit card debts, start fresh, go on to the next project. It's the American way."

He continued optimistically.

"You took risks, they didn't work out, the bankruptcy laws allow for that. We still try to do what we can to encourage entrepreneurs."

His enthusiasm was good, almost reassuring. I breathed a sigh of relief.

"It sounds like you can handle my situation."

I hadn't yet told him about the cancer since I didn't want that issue written up in the bankruptcy filing.

"Yes, I will take care of everything. First, my secretary will fill out all the forms. What you need to bring are all your credit card bills, a list of your assets, a current pay stub, and a budget of your expenses."

"I can get you that by the end of the week."

"Then we sign and file the paperwork with the court and get a date to meet with the bankruptcy trustee and finalize the filing. Typically, the credit card companies don't even show up at the meeting. Anyway, you don't have any money to pay them. So why worry?"

"I guess I was a little nervous." I wiped the sweat from my forehead. I suspect that it was the effects of steroid withdrawal as much as the financial information.

"My advice? Relax. Nothing to worry about. We see a lot of bankruptcies three years after a divorce. Of course, we get our fee before we file the paperwork."

"Sure, I have some money in the bank for that."

"Now keep in mind, after you file this, you can't declare bankruptcy for another six years."

"Fine, no problem."

A lot of people think of bankruptcy as a bad mark on your record, a frightening and humiliating experience. It's amazing how the cancer context makes some things irrelevant.

That late September afternoon, I walked into the courtyard and took a deep breath of the crisp Fall air. What a day! I

smiled to myself, 'I'm not really worried about my financial re-
cord six years from now. I wish I could care about it but I don't.
I probably won't live that long.' I guess all news is relative, and
I have to celebrate whatever positives I can.

That day, I counted Arnie as a really good development.

Waiting for Shin

For the first few days after the meeting with the bankruptcy attorney, I felt relaxed. I didn't worry about money at all. After all, I'm going to die anyway. It was a strange kind of relief. But as time went by, I became more and more agitated. Shin will be back soon. And I'd like to have a new plan for the future when she gets here.

Usually while I waited for her, I was full of hope and anticipation. She always made me the happiest guy in the world, no matter what we were doing.

But this time I felt different.

Here I was fifty-four years old, with incurable cancer and no money. What could I do for her now? What wrong turns had steered my life down this path of confusion and catastrophe?

My career is done, I have to find a new place to live, I have no way to catch up financially. My physical body is falling apart. And I had no significant accomplishments. I felt humiliated. The stress pains in my chest were telling my brain to be angry. Who made my life goals impossible? How can I go on?

Soon I would have to tell Shin face to face and admit my desperation and failure. There is nothing for me to give her. Nothing at all. Hope had left me. I was falling and falling without anything to stop me. I started to feel like the fishermen in the Perfect Storm with no fish ... only the emptiness of wind and water remained.

The Kirkland Café is about three blocks from the apartment in the opposite direction of Harvard University. One wall had a large screen TV showing baseball and football games to appeal to sports bar fans. But the rest of the place resembled a European style restaurant.

The bar area had a dark wooden counter that curved around the entrance to the kitchen. To the left of the bar, there were some floor-to-ceiling wooden bookcases with books that had been there for years. An English translation of Dante's 'Divine Comedy' was covered with dust but a couple of authors seemed to have gotten some recent attention — Nora Roberts and Sidney Sheldon. Hemingway and F. Scott Fitzgerald seemed misplaced next to a textbook on Calculus and Algebra.

The tables in the middle of the café were comfortable so I brought my books and laptop computer. I could work for several hours at a time and have a nice lunch or dinner. They served a wide variety of hot and cold sandwiches and an assortment of wines from around the world. I usually had Chardonnay from California or Cabernet Sauvignon from Australia.

When Shin was here, we didn't drink alcohol. Her bad experiences with her ex-husband's alcoholism had made it her enemy. She didn't like it at all and wanted me to avoid it as well.

But when she was gone, I had some flexibility. Under the circumstances, I felt that it was Ok to temporarily remove from my mind the list of serious problems facing me. Plus, the wine didn't conflict very much with the medicines that I was taking. Or so I thought.

On most evenings and weekend days, I dropped by the Kirkland Café. It was handy for food, soothing with the wine, and the people were friendly. I would read telephone industry articles or something about China or work on my laptop computer. If I didn't have the computer and had nothing to read, I would get a napkin and write lists of things to do or places to go before I died.

After three glasses of wine one Saturday afternoon, I had a Mexican quesadilla for lunch. Luckily, I still had a little cash to pay for all this, I thought. Although my money would eventually run out, it wasn't a major concern today.

For some reason, I have never really felt the need to accumulate lots of cash in a bank account. Whether for retirement or to pay for food next year, I suppose I always believed that I could figure it out when I got there. This was a risk of sorts but so far it had worked out well.

To me, money was only a way to buy a book or a gadget for the computer. I could use it to go to a symphony or go on a trip to Europe. But put a lot of it in a bank for the future? Saving for old age or retirement had always seemed like a foolish thing to do.

In a weird way, I was being proven right. If I had sacrificed and not traveled or not bought computer gadgets in order to pile up money for retirement, I would have missed experiences just to prepare for a future that I would never have. The official Social Security retirement age is sixty-two. The fact is that I will never see that birthday.

Perhaps impending death makes me a little cavalier about money. Maybe this is true of anyone with a terminal disease. But I did make sure that I had good health insurance when I started my job with IEC. And I do have enough money to pay for housing, food, and car for half a year. Thus I may appear to have a casual attitude but I do plan ahead.

What does seem disingenuous to me is dying people who chide visitors for paying too much attention to jobs and bank accounts. 'Pay attention to kids,' they say, 'watch the flowers and the sunsets.' There needs to be more balance in that counsel. My advice? 'Keep the job, keep the health insurance, get regular checkups at the doctor's office.' Sure, you can't predict when you'll die — but don't press your luck.

———

I walked outside a little unsteady. The sun was still out but the evening cool was settling in. I walked over to a nice little park near a large brick office building housing the American Social Sciences Organization. The park was open to the public so kids played with soccer balls, elderly people sat on the benches, and middle aged men and women exercised and ran.

I sat on a green park bench and felt good about myself. My new book on the Chinese economy was selling well in academic circles and I had given a dozen speeches to executives interested in doing business in China as the Beijing Olympics of 2008 approached. I had successfully transformed my knowledge of the cell phone industry in China to a general understanding of most of their major industries.

In TV interviews, I explained how the world economy would be China-centric for the foreseeable future. My passport was full of China visas and I was heading back to Shanghai next week. I could speak a fair amount of Mandarin Chinese and recognized some of the major written Chinese characters. I had finally made it. I considered myself a success.

A girl ran by shouting and chasing a dog. I caught myself.

My God, I'm going crazy. This Chinese thing was a dream. A total fiction, a pleasant hallucination. I suppose my subconscious wanted it to be true. Sure I could have done it with a little more time and effort, certainly if I did not have this cancer. But as a practical matter this whole thing was a mirage.

I had read where baseball pitchers visualize the game the night before, playing each batter in each inning — seeing the options and devising a strategy for the real game. Maybe this is what I had. But it seemed much worse. The pressure and the medication and the cancer were literally driving me crazy. I was terrified at the turns my mind was taking.

If I can't separate dreams from reality, I won't be able to fight the disease, get through the bankruptcy, and take care of

Shin. She has already made many decisions based on a plan to live with me in the United States.

Since she does not really have the possibility of taking a job here to make money, her financial future is in my hands. So I have to organize some new ways to make money next year. I better get a handle on things quickly. I stopped at the Kirkland Café for one more glass of wine before I went back to the apartment. The cold glass of Chardonnay seemed comforting and erased my thoughts for the moment.

When I got to the apartment, I planned out a European trip for Shin and myself. Southern Italy and the Greek Islands sounded like fun so I studied the guidebooks for Naples, Sicily, Athens, and Crete.

We could fly to Naples from Boston, then rent a car and drive to Palermo. From there we could take a ferry to Crete through a beautiful part of the Mediterranean. Then a plane to Athens, look at the Parthenon and the other sights there, then back to Boston.

I checked the airline and ferry schedules and looked on the Internet for possible hotels. I made lists of important tourist sights to see. This made my brain feel light and happy. I was optimistic. I went to sleep and did not once think about cancer.

When I woke up the next morning, the chemotherapy medicine side effects were back. I was light-headed, my hands shook, my back and legs ached, and my heartbeat seemed double what was normal.

According to a story I had seen on CNN Headline News, I had seventeen minutes to shower and eat breakfast. The promoter of the idea explained that your system was in a very receptive state for such activity for only a limited time after you got up. So I tried it, including using lemon-flavored shower gel to wake up my nose.

I still felt rotten and depressed. I didn't want to do anything. I decided to get out of the apartment. It seemed to be closing in on me, and my claustrophobia made it worse. I needed fresh air. I walked toward Harvard University, but at Sanders Hall I went left past the Fogg Museum towards the Charles River.

I felt short of breath and my legs hurt so I walked slowly. I remember all the old people with canes that I somehow felt sorry for or looked down upon in past years. Now it could be me next. Please, please let me walk normally through this cancer debacle.

I made it to the park along the Charles River. There is a stoplight there so I didn't have to try to cross Memorial Drive on my own. In my condition, I would not have made it alive.

I started to process all the options and alternatives before me. It was like a chess game, I thought, me against the world. My brain was spinning — a variety of different ways to get money at IEC from telecom projects, several things to do to finish the bankruptcy procedure, a list of things to cut from my monthly expenses, and several different ways to make money from my cancer predicament, including giving speeches to groups who wanted a first-hand account. The weight of the options and lists was oppressive.

I also have to tell Shin about all the new financial news when she gets here in October. Suddenly, I did not know and was not able to calculate what to do next. I was like a deer in front of the car headlights. Frozen, but still moving downhill at a rapid and relentless pace through the last part of my life.

It reminded me of the time one of my brothers and I were on a garage covered with snow. We miscalculated and wound up sliding down the ice-covered side of the slanted roof toward a fifteen-foot fall onto a picket fence and then to the ground. The time spent sliding lasted forever but there was nothing we could do, nothing to hold onto, no one to reach out to help us.

Now, thinking and dreaming, I was wandering around searching for solutions. I felt like I was walking through the clouds, floating aimlessly. I knew that I needed rest and maybe some food too.

I stopped at Pizzeria Uno in Harvard Square to get some food and rest. They had a nice area downstairs where I could usually find a newspaper. I had a club sandwich and a glass of wine to try to shake this sliding feeling. Eventually, I began to calm down.

Two graduate students were carrying on an animated conversation at the next table. They seemed so serious in this loud and crowded restaurant. A young woman in a white shirt and blue jeans was complaining to a guy in a suit.

"You're too materialistic," she said critically.

He was defensive, "What do you mean ... I just like to work. I want to get a great job and do lots of exciting things. That will probably result in a good salary. So what? What's the big problem?"

Her response was quieter, perhaps to avoid sounding like she was preaching.

"Eastern religions teach a principle of 'no possessions' ... only then can your mind be clear. Once you understand this, you can learn to care about other people. Then you can achieve true peace. I think that's a much more human approach."

"But the only way to feed people is to work hard on a farm and deliver it to the grocery store and sell it to shoppers. People who do that earn money that they might use to buy a house to live in. So possession, at least of money, is at the heart of where we live and how we eat. That sounds like a good thing for both of us."

She sat pensively for several minutes. "There is a saying, 'When wishes are few, the heart is happy. When desire ends, there is peace.' I really believe that."

The conversation was interesting to listen to. Years ago, I would have easily agreed with the guy. But now I desperately needed to achieve some kind of resolution of the deadly cancer in my blood and my dramatically changed life plan. Maybe the young woman made some sense ... that kind of thinking might have something for my troubled mind. I thought back to a visit to a monk in Thailand during the summer after my junior year in college.

———————

I still remember that day thirty years ago ... even at 5 am in the morning, it was incredibly hot and humid. A college friend of mine had arranged a meeting with a Buddhist monk at the Wat Po, one of the most famous temples in Bangkok. I had always been curious about Eastern religions, so I was glad to come along with him and see the temple and listen to what the monk had to say. Charlie had been in Thailand for a month and seemed to know his way around.

We had to take a motorcycle-style rikshaw called a *tuk-tuk* to get to the Chao Phraya, the main river that flows through Bangkok. Even this early in the morning there were plenty of people around, getting ready for the work of the day. The *tuk-tuk* ride was wild – the driver darted crazily in and out of speeding traffic on the expressway. But he seemed to avoid impending disaster easily as he turned around to describe the sights that we were zipping by.

He finally slowed down when we got to an area where vendors were selling all kinds of hot and cold food from carts on the side of the street. The smell of curry mixed with peanuts, chili peppers, coconut, and a variety of other things I couldn't identify.

I was still used to a donut and coffee for breakfast so nothing seemed appealing. Charlie motioned the driver to pull over.

"We have to buy some food to bring to the monk … that's the way they eat. Either they go out with bowls to beg from shops and houses near them, or people bring it to them to gain merit as they pass through this life into the next."

"That's right … Buddhists believe in reincarnation," I said, remembering a course in Asian history that I had taken in high school.

He picked out a curry-smelling dish and gave the vendor several bills. He also asked for something in Thai which I didn't understand. The vendor wrapped up the food and gave him a small burlap pouch full of coins.

"What's the bag of coins for?" I asked.

"Something we have to do at the temple. You'll see."

The driver dropped us off at a bustling dock along the Chao Phraya. The river and its offshoots affected most of Thai life here, from commerce to transportation even to washing clothes and dishes. The spiderweb-like system of waterways is so extensive that some early writers referred to Bangkok as the 'Venice of the East.'

What looked like a large canoe with a motor floated at the dock half-full of people. We paid and jumped in. Just before our destination, the boat slowed to a stop and a variety of smaller kayak-like boats paddled out to sell us flowers, souvenirs, and more food. Charlie bought a beautiful pink hibiscus flower to give the Buddha at the Wat Po temple where we were going.

"Flower gifts are a big deal in Thailand," he said as the boat pulled away to continue our journey.

"Yeah, I had a small garland made of a half dozen colored flowers on the door of my hotel room when I arrived."

The boat stop was several blocks from the temple so we got out and walked the rest of the way. The grounds of the Wat Po temple included a dozen buildings with steeply pointed terraced roofs. One building was a monastery where several hundred monks lived and operated a school that taught Buddhism to others. Inside another building, a large, gold reclining Buddha with huge feet dominated the main worship area. It must have been several hundred feet long and completely filled the small chapel we had crowded into.

"Don't point your toes at anyone or at Buddha," Charlie cautioned, "it's a big insult here. Put this flower over in the large container by the Buddha. It will gain merit for you in your next life."

We knelt down in a sitting position and studied the gold Buddha, the temple, and the other people there.

"Why are the statue's feet so big?" I whispered.

"The reclining Buddha depicts Buddha as he achieved Nirvana and died. On the soles of his feet are mother-of-pearl inserts representing 108 symbols of various Buddhist concepts."

We left the temple and headed for the classroom area of the monks' monastery. The sun was just starting to rise and the heat of early morning was almost intolerable. The increasing humidity made me start to sweat.

Charlie continued his explanation, "Monks get up at 5 am then meditate for an hour then walk out into the neighborhood to collect their food for the day. They don't plan for the future ... the whole philosophy seems to be based on what we would call 'one day at a time'."

A monk in a saffron orange-yellow robe recognized Charlie and motioned us into a small room with no furniture. We gave the traditional Thai greeting of putting our hands in a praying position near our mouths and bowed slightly. We sat on a yellow tile floor.

The monk closed his eyes in meditation. We tried to remain solemn as we waited. I wasn't very flexible so my legs started to hurt from sitting cross-legged on the floor.

Finally the monk looked at me and spoke.

"When you float like a branch in the river, you can meditate."

He thanked us for the curry and motioned us towards the door.

That was it. The lesson was over. I knew that he didn't know much English, so I didn't expect a long speech. But the shortness of the teaching was startling.

As we left, we spotted a student at the school. He knew some English, so we asked for an explanation of what the monk had said.

"One part of Buddhism is based on a rule of 'no possessions.' That's why the monks never own anything and only collect enough food for today. When you float in the river you're free from all the usual things that we strive for. Only this moment is important. You achieve a sense of content with where you are now. You have no control as you float with the river current and nothing else matters. That is the kind of clear-mind feeling you need to start the meditation that the Buddha teaches us."

We thanked him and headed off. Charlie steered me to another larger temple building with a bronze Buddha meditating in the lotus position. On the side were 108 small bronze bowls half-full of coins.

He pulled out the small bag of coins and gave me half. "Put one coin in each bowl. You start at the end by the incense and I'll start here. Make sure to do all 108 bowls ... that will ensure you good health."

Then we left.

I had a good time touring the rest of Bangkok with Charlie before I headed back home. But I didn't think much about the monk's lesson after that. Back then, it didn't make much sense to me. I had spent a lot of time in school already. When I graduated, I wanted to get a good job, make some money, and raise a family. Floating aimlessly didn't seem like much fun at the time.

————————

I left the restaurant and started down Broadway to the apartment. I wondered if reincarnation could actually happen. Would I really leave this life and come back as someone else? Was it possible to live one day at a time without any plan for the future? Should I concentrate on floating peacefully down a river?

There must be some reason that the memory of the Thai monk still stuck with me. At least my searching seemed to be giving me some promising ideas. After all, anything was pleasanter than my current health and finances.

Unexpectedly, my chest started to tighten with pain. It was like a panic attack but it sometimes happened after I ate when I was on steroids. It was extremely uncomfortable and forced me to sit down at some tables outside the Broadway Marketplace, a neighborhood grocery store and delicatessen. After ten minutes of rest, I felt a little better, so I walked inside.

They had a nice selection of wines and since I didn't feel like working, I figured 'what the heck, why not? Shin would be here soon, so enjoy the wine now while I had a chance.'

I bought a bottle of Merlot from a place in the state of Washington. I didn't know that grapes would grow that far North, but past experience told me that the wine was quite good.

The last time I was in that grocery store, Shin and I were buying apples and bananas and grapes. That was before I knew I had incurable cancer. Shin had kindly taken on the mission of helping me reduce my weight, and I was cooperating fully. I easily lost ten pounds following her advice and eating the great Korean food that she cooked sometimes. Now cancer had put that program on hold and our focus was keeping me alive for as long as possible. What a change!

I was overwhelmed by the long list of things that I had to do, all the choices, all the alternative ways to make money. 'Relax,' I told myself, 'you'll be dead soon.' I guess these things should probably be taken with a grain of salt. But wait, I wanted so badly to take good care of Shin and Dan and Amy after I left. I need to, I want to, I will. My heart ached. My situation seemed hopeless. But I couldn't let it hurt the ones I loved.

———————

By the time I got to the apartment, the world map with China in the center seemed like a great relief. At least I knew something about the coming importance of China in the world economy. I started up my laptop computer and logged into a website by a professor at California State University.

It had Mandarin Chinese lessons with both the Chinese characters and regular characters with indications of the tones so that I could attempt the complicated pronunciation. The site also had MP3 audio files to listen to the lessons by a native Chinese speaker. It was the best I had seen, better than the many books and CDs that I had purchased over the years. I had a glass of wine and started at the first page.

"Hello. My name is Li. I am a teacher. Goodbye." I had a good ear for languages and could imitate the pronunciation pretty closely. Wait a minute. What good would knowledge of Chinese do after I was dead? How would this help defeat cancer or take care of Shin? I guess it was fun. But why was I questioning everything that I was doing or thinking? The cancer and the medicine and the financial problems were driving me crazy. I stopped studying Chinese.

I walked to the bedroom but I forgot why I had gone there. I walked back to the living room to get something. What was it? I couldn't remember. I had another glass of wine to calm myself down.

I started listening to some music by Albinoni. Most of it was light and airy Baroque concertos. But his most famous piece, Adagio in G Minor for organ and strings, was quite sad.

As an experiment I laid down on the floor on my back. I folded my hands on my stomach and closed my eyes. It seemed relaxing. I hadn't seen many dead people but those that I had seen looked like this. My God, I really was losing my mind. Was this depression or insanity? Or was I just being stupid? 'Get out of the apartment,' I told myself.

———

My favorite hangout, the Kirkland Café, had closed early so I walked several blocks further down Beacon Street to another restaurant called the Thirsty Scholar. It had a crowded bar on the right and a blackboard with a list of all the beers that they served. It seemed to be run by Irish immigrants so there were plenty of European beers, including the famous Guinness.

Soccer was on the TVs and the tables on the left were full of people eating a late dinner. Guinness has a strange taste at first but it was quite strong. So, after a couple of pints, I was feeling no pain. The place was packed with students celebrating the weekend.

On some nights, they had a contest where the object was to answer general knowledge questions about politics, science, literature, movies, business, sports, and world events. Bar patrons would form groups of three or four, choose a name, and collaborate on submission of answers to the questions.

It was a great marketing move, and the place was usually packed. I didn't sign up with anybody at the beginning but I knew several answers after they started so I helped a group at the bar. They were called the 'The Lost Generation.'

"Who started an airline, a music label, a soda company, and a cellular telephone carrier in the last ten years?" Richard Branson.

"What is the name of the 1953 movie that starred Gregory Peck and Audrey Hepburn?" Roman Holiday.

"Name the author of the popular Buddhist book, 'Siddhartha'." Herman Hesse.

I won a Rolling Rock t-shirt for my efforts. At least I was good for something. Another beer to celebrate.

During the five block walk back to the apartment, an airplane flew through the dark sky. Maybe that's where I would go after I die. Constantly circling the earth looking down at the water, the snow covered mountains, the sandy deserts, the patchwork of farms, big cities every now and then, and lots and lots of clouds. Sunrise, sunset, never landing, always in the air.

The day was almost done. I felt like I was caught in this huge swirling whirlpool of white water. It was dragging me around and around and down and down. My life was going down the toilet. 'Please make this stop,' I prayed, 'please.' I wondered desperately, 'How much longer till Shin arrives to talk to me, take care of me, and hold me?'

Floating Downstream

Sun shining in the window woke me up. I didn't feel rested. I was trying to remember what I did last night, but I couldn't. I was in bed with my eyes open, but my body would not move.

The side effects seemed no longer connected to the chemotherapy medication — they were now living inside of me permanently, swirling in my blood and making me insane. My body was shaking and exhausted so much that I could barely get up. I opened the refrigerator to get some orange juice but instead I had a couple glasses of wine.

After that I felt less shaky. Then I got on the computer to check for emails from Shin. Nothing. Of course, now I remembered … she was finishing her daughter's wedding in Korea then flying to Washington D.C. to attend a friend's wedding. A quick visit there before she gets to Boston on the 12th. She was probably traveling to DC right now. I sent her my classic email message, 'Everything fine, everything on schedule.' 'What a lie,' I thought. 'But why worry her before she gets here?'

My cancer had definitely started to change my perception and judgment. Sometimes time was frozen still — the next minute, days passed in the blink of an eye. What had I accomplished while she was gone?

I missed her so terribly but I was also terrified at the thought of talking with her when she arrives. Luckily, I had some time to prepare. I knew I had to do some marketing emails for consulting projects today, but decided to do it from my computer at the apartment. Then I could start to clean the house and buy groceries. I sent an email to my secretary that I would be working at home.

Suddenly, I started to see stars and sparkles in my eyes while looking at the computer screen. I took off my glasses. The sparkles stayed. They were pleasant but disturbing. They stayed when I looked around the room.

I knew they were connected to the anti-cancer medications. Not good, I thought. I had these once several months before, so I knew it wasn't the after-effects of the wine. When I first started the Thal-Dex drugs, they had occurred for several days when I was working on the computer at my office. Then they went away. Were they back to stay now?

After a couple more glasses of wine, it was lunchtime and I was hungry. Shin had always encouraged me to eat at home to keep my weight down. But she would be here soon and I couldn't resist take-out food that day.

Dial-A-Pizza, a square white building on Beacon Street, sold a dozen kinds of pizza and submarine sandwiches. Robert, the owner, was about my age with gray hair, a white apron, and a ready smile. He was always talkative so I had told him about Shin and my visits to Korea. He had been there before too, probably in the military.

The place was handy when all I wanted was a sandwich to take back to the apartment. I usually ordered a small Italian submarine with hot peppers and no pickles. I bought a pepperoni pizza there once but by the time I had walked the three blocks to the apartment, it was cold. So I usually stuck to my submarine sandwich favorite.

Just down the street is a park bench outside of the Spanish tapas restaurant called Dali for people waiting for a seat. I sat down to eat my submarine sandwich and enjoy the warm sun.

From there, I could see a large billboard advertising an SUV sitting on a mountain top against a blue sky scattered with white puffy clouds. Maybe that's where I would go after I die — live in the car and watch the clouds go by. I'd like to bring pictures of Shin and Dan and Amy and keep them with me on the dashboard.

Also recordings of them talking on my Sony portable digital voice recorder so I could listen when I wanted to. Plus Shin singing all my favorite Korean songs. And a large supply of batteries too, I thought.

I finished the sandwich and was now thirsty. The Wine and Cheese Cask on the corner of Kirkland and Beacon, was only a half a block away. They sold two dozen kinds of cheese, olives, fresh bread, deli sandwiches to go, and a large selection of wines from around the world. They had inexpensive champagne of good quality in a refrigerated case just past the deli counter. I bought two bottles.

I headed back to the apartment, drank a bottle of champagne, and watched the movie 'Top Gun'. I had always wanted to fly airplanes but somehow never got organized enough to take lessons. Perhaps it was the lack of money, perhaps it was the lack of time. Anyway, I had to be content with watching movies and flying in the passenger seats. Actually there are a lot of things I never will do. It felt like time was closing in on me.

The TV came on automatically when the movie was over. It was showing interviews of professional golfers before a major tournament. Most were modest but optimistic about their chances. 'I can win this,' was their unspoken claim. My first inclination was to change the channel. I had to get used to settling for losing. I was torn and confused. What had happened to my ambition? Why couldn't I get up off the floor and make a comeback? So what if I had just missed an easy putt and lost a close tournament. Get back in the running, don't let cancer close out my career. But my stomach churned with doubt. I finally changed the channel.

To comfort myself, I watched another favorite movie, 'Lost in Translation' with Bill Murray and Scarlett Johansson in Tokyo. It reminded me of the first time that I met Shin on a tour bus and we had talked nonstop for eight hours around Tokyo. She was so beautiful and amazing! I wish I could go back to that warm June day. I would scoop her up into my arms and fly away to paradise and disappear from this world forever and ever.

At this moment, I missed her desperately, even though I have such bad news to tell her when she gets here. I long to hold her small warm hand in mine to feel the excitement, the hope, the reassurance, and the confidence.

I walked over to the bench in the park next at the Social Science building. It was only three blocks from the apartment and I needed the fresh air. An athletic guy who looked like he was resting sat down next to me. He looked prosperous and wore nice running clothes. He must have been in his thirties. Not overweight, he looked pretty healthy. I wish I could say the same about myself.

He began to talk about his recent visit to Egypt. His voice was enthusiastic and he seemed well-informed. I could see that he was excited to tell somebody about his trip so I listened.

"Cairo is the most amazing place in the world. The streets are full of traffic and commerce. Deliveries of soap, groceries, industrial goods, wood, construction supplies, milk, soda, water, books, computers, you name it."

"And most of it on the back of motorbikes with a small bracket on the back. There is every kind of small shop you could imagine and marketplaces and street vendors everywhere. Amazing!"

"But the best thing about the city is the Cairo Museum just off the main square downtown. They claim it is the best archeological museum in the world, and I believe it with all the stuff from the pyramids from three and four thousand years ago. Important statues, stones with hieroglyphic writing, and ceramic and gold jars which contained food and drink for the Pharaoh in the afterlife. The museum has things from all of the major pyramid burial sites. Fantastic place to go!"

He continued, so I listened to his curious observations.

"I went out to the pyramids at Giza, took a camel ride around the sand and watched the sun set. What an experience! But the most interesting thing to me was their belief that the Pharaoh needed all kinds of supplies to take with him on his next journey after he had left this life. They put in statues, books, boats, food, drink, furniture, and plenty of gold. Some of the pyramids even have shafts designed for his quick escape to the stars."

"So they spent thousands of man-years constructing these pyramids and creating an inside which the guide now calls the 'dark and mysterious world of the dead.' But it wasn't mysterious to them at all. Here it was three thousand years ago and they were sure that our life on earth was just part one of a longer journey. Tell me, what ever happened to that philosophy?"

I had been listening quietly with my eyes closed, imagining the visions of ancient Egypt that he was painting. I looked at him to see if his question needed a comment or an answer.

No one was there. Where had he gone? He was just here a minute ago. But no one was in the park. It was totally deserted. Wait ... where was I anyway? I was actually sitting on my couch watching TV. The Discovery Channel was running a special show on Egypt. There was no way that any real person had just been sitting next to me. And I wasn't outside at all ... I was in the apartment. Oh No! Jesus Christ! The whole conversation was imaginary. And I didn't even know where I was!

What is happening? Real enough in its information but ... my God ... I had probably dozed off watching TV. This was really pathetic! Shin would be here soon and I should be preparing.

Was this a cancer medicine hallucination or alcohol or both? Of course, I do want to go to see the Pyramids some day. But this event was not comforting. I felt bewildered and confused. I was losing my mind. This was not the usual effect of alcohol on my system. It was terrifying … I had gone downhill so rapidly!

On a deeper note though, now that I only had a year or so left, this idea of going somewhere in the afterlife with some key things seemed appealing. Certainly my nice collection of a thousand portrait photos of Shin that I could look at while I was continuing my journey. 'Wait. Stop,' I told myself, 'Go to bed and get some real sleep. Now!'

I sat down at the table and turned on the computer. I looked up the word 'afterlife' in Google. Most of the search results listed Buddhism. There it was again. When I put my head down on the computer keyboard to rest, I knew I was getting close to the edge.

———————

The next day when I woke up, I smelled chocolate chip cookies cooking in the oven. My mother used to make those on special occasions and when she wanted to cheer everyone up. I wandered into the kitchen.

No mother, no cookies, no smells.

In reality, my mother and I weren't that close. When I called to tell her that I had cancer, she had acted really weird.

"It's nothing, don't worry, it will go way. By the way, I'm remodeling the house…"

I was shocked at her response.

She had rambled on, as if she were talking to a distant acquaintance. I guess I expected more comforting thoughts from my own mother. Anyway, no big deal, most people don't know how to react to my deadly cancer. Plus I hadn't called or written for years. Why should I expect a dramatically new relationship now?

I drank the other bottle of champagne with some orange juice and went for a walk. Without Shin, the walls of the small apartment were closing in on me again.

I sat at the same park bench at the Social Science Building. It was quieter than the one by Dali's on the street. I started to imagine what was going on inside of my blood. It was like a sci-fi movie I once saw where the explorer took an adventurous submarine trip inside the human body and encountered all kinds of enemies and dangers.

Usually plasma cells live on battleships in your blood. When you get a disease like flu, the ships wake up the plasma cells and they fight the disease with antibodies. When they are done they go back to sleep.

Unfortunately the enemy Myeloma cells sneak into the bone marrow and take over your plasma cells. Then, the altered plasma cells keep multiplying and crowding out your regular red and white blood cells. At this point, they seem to have forgotten how to go to sleep.

All of a sudden, my arms felt funny where the needles had gone in to do the pheresis to clean my blood. This battle seemed to be raging inside of me at that moment. It made my arms ache.

My imagination continued to spin.

Multiple Myeloma basically creates a very powerful and effective sabotage mission in your blood. Eventually your bone marrow is full of enemy cancer cells giving out the wrong orders and your bones start to develop painful bumps and fractures.

Your energy is drastically reduced and your risk of infection is much higher than for well people. Since it is everywhere in your bone marrow and blood, a local operation similar to that used for some kinds of cancer is impossible.

When your blood fills up with unwanted proteins from the Myeloma cells, the battle ships are close to losing the war. Then you don't have much time left.

Now my legs were getting weak. Frantic, I looked for swelling in my ankles to check for blood clots which might give me a heart attack. Nothing yet.

Unfortunately, no one knows how to prevent the enemy cancer's sabotage program. The various medicines are like spies trying to sneak around and figure out a way to defeat the bad Myeloma army. If one kind of spy doesn't work, we try another kind. If you find a spy that works, you take that medicine for a while, dealing with the side effects as they occur.

Eventually, the only thing left to do is called a stem cell transplant. This rescue mission sneaks out some good stem cells out of the bone marrow and puts them in the freezer. Then they drop a nuclear bomb into you, destroying all the blood cells and bone marrow.

Since the bomb has obliterated your blood system, the only hope is the stuff in the freezer. They put the refrigerated stem cells back into you and watch everything grow back. The battleships work again and the new plasma cells are hopefully back to what they were several years ago. Since the disease is incurable, there are still some Myeloma cells around waiting to grow back again. So you might gain a couple of years with the transplant.

Unfortunately, the nuclear bomb makes you into a vegetable for at least three months, with no energy and no immune system. Recovery is a long slow process ... perhaps as much as a year. And most people have to start taking chemotherapy drugs again after the transplant to control the Myeloma cells that are left.

Thinking about the war inside my blood and bones made me exhausted and demoralized. Most people don't have to deal with this. Why do I?

I stopped at the Café for a sandwich and a glass of wine. A guy at the bar wearing a Harley-Davidson leather motorcycle jacket had written the letters 'H.A.T.E' on four knuckles of his left hand. On the right hand knuckles he had written 'L.O.V.E'.

It reminded me of an old-time movie where a scary minister showed two little kids a frenzied fight between the two hands in a futile attempt to get them to come to church.

I imagined the same thing about my life now. Maybe one hand was cancer and the other was cured. Maybe one hand was wealth and the other bankruptcy. Perhaps pessimism vs. hope, or loneliness vs. Shin here. Most likely it was life vs. death. These letters actually fit on the five fingers if I really was crazy enough to find a pen and write them there.

What brought me this panic and fear which seemed to be driving me more and more to alcohol? The main worry was the failure of the financial picture that I would have to tell Shin about. The reduction in the IEC salary would have an immediate impact on our budget. She was not a big spender at all so that might not be too much of a problem. But the bankruptcy would also be a disappointment to her. And now it would be impossible to travel to see new things which we both enjoyed a lot.

Plus, when she saw me in person, she would realize that the cancer medications were definitely producing negative side effects. With a red face and bloated stomach, shaky hands, disorientation, unsteady walk, shortness of breath, and mood swings, I didn't feel very cute and lovable.

No doubt about it, I was disillusioned and depressed. And it was frightening. I had never experienced this in my life before cancer. I felt that I was dragging Shin into more problems than she had ever dreamed of. Maybe she wouldn't want to come on this more dangerous journey.

I had another glass of wine to console myself and attempt to ease my fears. I don't remember if it was white or red wine, but it tasted good.

Walking home that night, it was dangerous to cross the street. It was not that busy but my slow walk combined with medication dizziness and the effects of the alcohol made me frightened of all the moving cars. My clothes were dark and the busses were always in a hurry. I walked down to the designated crosswalk and hoped for some cars to notice me and stop and wave me across.

What a pitiful change from several months ago. What a downfall from my days before cancer!

All of a sudden, I burst out crying on the sidewalk. It was as if someone had reached inside me and turned on the kitchen faucet. I couldn't control myself. I desperately needed love and hope and optimism.

Most important, I required the strength and courage to move forward. At this moment, I just did not have it.

When I got back to the apartment, I remembered what Shin told me to do if I were sad. I got out a white board that we used to write examples of Chinese, Japanese, and Korean.

I turned it over and titled it "Things That are Good about My Situation." I wrote down a) I am not dead, b) Shin is coming soon, c) I have an excellent cancer doctor, d) My health insurance seems to be paying for everything, e) I still have a place to live, a car, clothes, and food, f) I have lots of interesting books to read someday, and g) I have a nice laptop computer connected to the Internet. I recall hearing somewhere that this kind of list was a start to curing depression. I don't remember if there was a prescription for curing hallucinations and craziness. Probably not.

I leaned back in bed and closed my eyes but I could not sleep. My mind was still spinning. I tried to get up to watch a movie or do physical exercises or get on the Internet.

I could not move. I was paralyzed. I was in a nightmare and someone was sending me thoughts that I was required to think about.

I have incurable cancer. But so what? Lots of people do. I may die in a year or two. Who cares? Lots of people are not here anymore. They are gone somewhere else. That's where I was heading.

What had I done to help others out in my life? Suddenly, I was getting a sort of angst and regret that I should have done more for others. Sure, I had focused on family and Shin but others had not really been in the picture. If I had been a better volunteer would that have saved me from cancer? Of course not, yet I still became tormented by what I could have done with my life, but did not.

I heard music from the apartment upstairs. They seemed to be playing the same jazz song over and over again. With CD players these days, that is easy to do. Then I heard people talking, but they seemed closer to me than upstairs. They were in my living room.

I could not hear what they were saying — anyway only the rental agency had a key. But maybe someone had gotten concerned about my condition and called an ambulance and they had gotten the key.

Eventually, I was able to get out of bed to see what was going on. No people in the apartment. No talking upstairs. No music playing anywhere. Nothing.

The whole thing was another mysterious hallucination. With the multiple days of little food and lots of alcohol, I was deteriorating rapidly. On top of that, the already serious side effects of the medications were combining to further worsen my condition.

I was scheduled to meet Shin at the airport soon so I needed to get organized quickly.

I started making lists of things to tell her one at a time so as not to overwhelm her. Cancer stuff, career change stuff, bankruptcy stuff, IEC telecom stuff, how I will cut expenses, where to move, how to slow down to let the medications work.

I was overwhelmed and dejected. What master of destiny had decided to wreck my life by giving me all these challenges at the same time?

I decided to go on a quick walk outside to wake myself up. Then I could do at least one thing on my list. As I opened the door to go out of my apartment, I was engulfed by a ten foot wave of salt water.

It knocked me backwards onto the deck of the 40 foot sailboat. The boat was reeling in the storm, ready to capsize at any minute. I was in charge and was trying to lower the sails. The rest of the people with me were less experienced and so terrified that they were useless as helpers.

I sent them to the cabin below so they could not see the true danger of the situation. I got the sails half down before a line jammed. The wind and waves were whipping the boat around like a toy in a bathtub.

We had to keep the bow pointed into the constantly shifting wind. If we got stuck sideways to the waves, we would most certainly swamp the boat, capsize and drown. I tried to use the outboard motor to help do this but the water washed over the top of the engine and shorted out the controls. A constant spray of salt water covered my face.

"Jesus Christ!" A wave three stories high was heading for us and I did not have time to get the boat pointed correctly. It would cover us with enough water to make it impossible to control the boat further.

It was time to alert the others that we had to ditch and to be prepared to head off in the small rubber lifeboat. As skipper, I had failed to get us through the storm and back to port safely. True, it had come up suddenly and wasn't predicted but I had always taken pride in my ability to sail through the rough weather. Now this was the end of the line.

The wave approached steadily as I tried to point the bow into it. The wind increased rapidly hitting the half-down sails and pushing the boat in the opposite direction that I wanted to steer.

The wave was here, smashing everything in its path. It swept me off the boat as it filled the cabin below with water. The line that held me to the boat snapped and I was thrown into the cold and turbulent waters of the North Atlantic.

The salt water taste in my mouth had always been pleasant — reminding me of vacations and fun. This time it was deadly. I was drowning. And I had failed the others who were now stuck in the cabin waiting to drown as well.

———————

I looked at my watch ... It was still before midnight. Good. I decided to have a couple more beers at the Thirsty Scholar one last time before Shin arrives. The place was packed with people celebrating and laughing and visiting with friends. I drank a pint of Guinness. I felt a part of a lost generation. Where were those books by Hemingway and F. Scott Fitzgerald anyway?

There was plenty of light in this part of the bar. Ah, those were at the Kirkland Café and they were closed now. But the feeling that I was in a club all by myself hung on. Sure, there were other people who were also members but not likely in this bar now.

It was bizarre, looking at these people like they were all speaking Russian and I couldn't understand or relate at all. In a weird way, I was different and special. I was dying sooner than them.

I had another Guinness and asked the bartender for some napkins and a pen. Both of my hands were shaking — but hey, I was drinking beers, so who's worried?

I wrote lists of good things, bad things, things to do, happy memories, mistakes that I had made, napkin after napkin. When I was ready to go, I studied what I had written. They were illegible and incomprehensible, all of them. I was finally defeated. I threw the napkins in the trash as I left.

I felt light-headed and dizzy. I desperately needed to get some sleep before Shin gets here. I had to pick her up the day after tomorrow. My mind raced to the typical airport scenery.

All of a sudden my brain put me on one of those moving walkways. I zipped by — watching the people and stores and lights. Only here I was heading to the apartment. Down Beacon Street two blocks past a movie rental store, a restaurant, and a bank, then left on Kirkland Street past the Spanish restaurant, the Café, a drycleaners, and several blocks of apartment buildings.

My moving escalator trip passed by groups of people heading home. Even the ones who were alone were talking to friends on a cell phone. When I got to my apartment, I hopped off the moving sidewalk and walked upstairs. I knew I was in the right apartment because of the maps of Europe and China on the walls. I set the alarm and went to bed.

Over these last several weeks, I had adopted a phrase that I said each night, 'Just stay alive until morning.' Pathetic and tragic, I know. But it was the way I felt.

———

In the morning, I vowed to have no alcohol that day so that I could dry out before Shin arrives. But first, I had to get out of the apartment. I decided on a trip to the Wellness Community, a place for cancer patients to meet each other, compare notes on medical treatments, discuss problems, and cheer each other up. They also had counselors, regular meetings, a nice library, and a conference room with peaceful views of trees and a famous stone bridge.

A receptionist at the front desk recognized me and said, "You must be here for the class on meditation. They're in the big classroom around the corner."

"Thanks," I said, surprised at the good timing.

This was one of the many services that they provided free to cancer patients. They had courses in exercise, cooking, flower arranging, and even one that focused on humor. I decided to head in to try to learn something new. I sat down on a clean white rug with five other cancer patients. A large mural of a bright orange Lotus flower hung calmly on the wall.

"Hi. I'm Anna. Just make yourselves comfortable. As usual, I will start with a teaching to think about during our session. Then we'll talk about how to sit, breathe, and meditate."

She was slight and quiet but her eyes sparkled as she continued in a confident voice, "Under the floor of a poor man's house is a treasure. But since he does not realize it, he spends his life thinking he is poor."

Interesting, I thought. It reminded me of my encounter with the Thai monk so many years ago.

"Today I want you to look for the treasure inside of yourself that you don't realize is there. Now let's talk about your position. Most of you are beginners so I don't want you to sit cross-legged unless it's easy for you ... just sit or kneel comfortably. Close your eyes and let the tension exit your body."

I sat with my legs straight and my back against the wall. I had never been very flexible, even before cancer. I suppose I could try something more athletic but I wanted to focus on what she had to say.

"Breathing right is critical. First observe each breath as it enters and exits your mouth. Now gradually lengthen it and deepen it ... you should see your chest and your abdomen move. The oxygen is flowing within you."

"Let go of emotions. Happiness, sadness, anger, anxiety, and boredom will float away from you. Treat the thoughts that enter your brain like a slide show. Don't get involved, just click each one away as soon as it enters. Your objective is clarity. Focus on nowness. Forget about the past and don't worry about the future. Nothing matters but this moment."

I started to relax.

"But don't sleep, the purpose is to gain insight at the same time you reduce stress. That's the hard part. Let each breath clear your mind and open your heart."

After several minutes, it was hard to stop my mind from planning ahead, as if I needed something else to do while watching TV.

"Ok, I can tell you're thinking too much. Your minds are too active. Let's advance one step. Keep your eyes closed. You are careening along in a crashing river with no control but no danger. The current deftly swirls you past the rocks and branches. Let yourselves peacefully float downstream in this whirlpool. You will not be harmed."

This seemed to work. I wasn't bored. I felt the stress leaving my body. Time passed as I let the scenery of the river entertain me.

After a half hour, Anna whispered, "It is time now, open your eyes."

For the first time in a year, I felt like a success. I hadn't thought about cancer at all. I had learned something new. I was able to control my mind to help change my perspective ... even if it was only for an hour. A pleasant calm seemed to surround me.

Without alcohol, new strength flowed inside of me to help confront my difficulties.

I headed home in peace. My physical body was still a wreck but I felt that I had accomplished something important in my mind. I knew that I was still sick but at least I had finally experienced a glimmer of hope.

The Rescue

The gray morning brought a steady drizzle. It was an October rain, not freezing, but not warm like summer either. I felt like crying. The medications had taken over again and the stress of Shin's impending arrival was overwhelming. My head was spinning and my hands were shaking. I was sweating like crazy. My heart was breaking with failure and frustration. The Buddhist calm that I had experienced yesterday seemed a distant, faded memory.

I sat down on the couch holding my cell phone trying to figure out the best way to get Shin from the airport. Now I realized the stupidity of what I had done. I didn't eat much, drank a lot, didn't accomplish anything.

How did I get into that rut? And why? Besides that, I was hardly sleeping at all.

When I looked in the mirror, I couldn't believe what I had done to myself. I was a physical and mental wreck ... devastated and distraught.

Only one good thing — I did take my medicines on time. But I looked really awful. And my head was still spinning. I shouldn't have had all that wine and beer. A nice shower helped a little, but the spray of water couldn't postpone the inevitable.

Only a couple hours left before I would have to tell Shin all the bad news. I knew that it would be dangerous to try to drive to the airport to pick her up. Nothing had gone right so far since Shin had left. My brain was just too fuzzy and a car accident would just complicate matters.

True, I could take a taxi there and then we could take a taxi home but that did not make too much sense with my current financial problems. So I just waited for time to pass. I knew that Shin would call my cell phone when I did not show up at the airport. Then I would just tell her to take a cab to the apartment.

I was so nervous, I almost dropped my phone when it rang at 8:30. She probably thought that I was at the airport somewhere looking for her.

"David, where are you?'

"I'm still at the apartment. I was feeling a little sick so I stayed here. Can you take a taxi? Then we can talk and eat and play and hug and kiss when you get here."

"Of course, I'll see you in a half hour. Is something wrong with you, David?" Her voice was tense with worry and uncertainty.

"Oh, just bad side effects from the medicines, I think."

I stood by the window waiting for Shin to arrive. I was hopeless, sluggish, defenseless but desperately wanted to see Shin. She was my only hope.

Soon a taxi came slowly down the street and stopped. Suddenly, she was in front of the apartment with her suitcases. My beautiful angel, she looked so young and pretty! I rushed downstairs … I was so happy to finally see her.

When we hugged and kissed on the sidewalk, the warmth of her body was like heaven. Her magic smile was so comforting and calming. Of course I had not forgotten all the serious things that we had to talk about. But for this brief moment, I was transported back to days when we had no cares in the world. Looking at the stars in the desert sky in California, we had planned out a future of endless possibilities.

I took her hand, "My dearest darling, you are finally here. I missed you so so much."

The rain soaked us but she didn't seem to want to move. She studied my condition in shock, not knowing what to say or do. After a minute, she started to cry. I had forgotten that she had not really seen my red puffy face, bloated stomach, and shaky hands. She seemed to be finally realizing that I was really dying. She was stunned.

"Oh my David, I will take good care of you now," she said weakly.

Although my legs were unsteady, my arms were still quite strong. So I grabbed her heavy suitcase and awkwardly started up the stairs. She was protesting, "Let me do that. You look like you need to rest."

We finally got the luggage up the two flights of stairs and into the apartment. But I could see from her face that she was still in shock. What was it? I ducked into the bathroom quickly to see how I looked. I couldn't see myself in the mirror. What I saw was a dying ghost.

We hadn't really talked much about my condition when she was at the weddings. Whenever she asked me how I was doing I had said 'I'm fine, don't worry about me, take your time' and also my classic email messages — 'Everything is on schedule.' Now she could see the truth.

"Sit here David, please calm down a little."

When she held my hand, she burst into tears. She was trying to talk but her voice couldn't come out. She just let the tears roll down her cheeks for a while.

"David, I think the cancer is taking you away from everybody including me. I can see that you are getting sicker, a lot worse than I expected. Oh David, you should have told me how rapidly your condition was going down hill. I could have come earlier. What does Dr. Portinari say about your cancer?"

"Shin, I am so sorry about that, but I didn't want to tell you until you came here. I knew you had a lot of work to do for your daughter's wedding. I didn't want to interrupt that."

My mind was trying to thank her for coming to take care of me, but I couldn't finish what I was trying to say. Now tears were coming down my face too. She held my shaky hands more tightly.

"Shin, let's just lay down on the bed for a while."

The dark yellow quilt with red roses and the royal blue pillows with bunches of pink and white flowers that she had prepared for me before she had gone were always comforting. Now even more, they were a welcome relief. At last, I have her here but I still did not know how to tell her all the bad news. 'What's good about my mess?' I wondered to myself. But only one thought was in my mind, 'please don't go away Shin, stay with me'.

We both cried, sensing the desperation of the situation. Neither of us bothered to wipe the tears away. I knew that I had a very hard day ahead of me.

This was the time to be strong, unsentimental, and focused — but I couldn't get rid of the thought that 'I'm such a failure ... I have wrecked my life financially and now the cancer is destroying my body.' Yet I had to get ready to take the next steps to fix the situation and begin to develop a plan for Shin and myself. And this moment was no time for weakness and feeling sorry for myself.

We laid down next to each other in the bright colors of the covers ... a futile attempt to cheer us up. I was trying to draw strength from her presence but I didn't know what she was thinking. She closed her eyes to rest for a while.

Her face was so sweet and gentle but her forehead was creased with worry and stress. What a difference from the photos of her that I had taken in Italy several years ago! In that warm sun, she had looked like a beautiful young angel without a care in the world. The lightest breeze could have sent her swirling into the air, laughing and singing. Now, destiny had given us a whole new set of challenges.

Eventually she opened her mouth, "David what did you have for breakfast?"

Her question was unexpected. I had thought she was still in shock from seeing my appearance.

"Nothing yet." I said.

"I will cook some rice soup with milk and carrots. That will give us some strength and be good for our stomachs. It will probably calm you down a little bit too."

The hot plain soup comforted us as we settled in the living room surrounded by the maps and the books and the classical music CDs. But the stress and the hot liquid made me sweat.

"I have bad news about some things, my darling."

I wiped my forehead with a blue patterned handkerchief that she had given me last year.

She turned anxiously, "About the cancer?"

"Not really, well yeah, I guess it's all connected. The good news is that the Thal-Dex medicine is definitely working against the cancer. My IgG level, which measures the bad proteins in my blood, keeps going down. So that is good. But the side effects have gotten bad enough to make me conclude that my professional consulting career is over."

"What do you mean?"

"Some days my face is so puffy and red that I really can't go into the office. If I went to a client to give a report or convince them to hire me to do a consulting project, they would know that I was sick. They would pick someone else to do it. Even if they didn't know that I had cancer, this would be a natural reaction. Many times when I think I look acceptable, other people at IEC look twice at me and ask about my health."

She breathed with a little bit of relief.

"Oh, well that's pretty much what you predicted earlier. For a smart person like you, changing careers is not that big a deal. I sort of noticed that you were having difficulties with the consulting. You told me months ago, when I was here, the marketing wasn't going well. In fact, what I was worried about at that time was after a customer had hired you, what if you wouldn't have enough strength and endurance to actually do the project. You should take care of your health first, and then find a career that matches your capabilities with the cancer medications and go from there."

Shin had changed into light pink corduroy pants, a smooth green long sleeve shirt and a fuzzy red sweater vest. I was wearing brown shorts and a navy blue polo shirt. She said that I looked thinner when I wore dark clothes, so I was trying to impress her in any small way that I could. But what a difference between us! She is slim, healthy, so beautiful, and ready to go have fun — but me, puffy face, overweight, weak, shaky hands, and an unsteady walk ... not to mention the serious cancer in my blood.

I continued to talk, "Another bad financial thing happened over the last couple of weeks that I couldn't discuss with you at all because you were at the weddings. What happened was that IEC claimed that they had overpaid me for the last ten months. So now they have cut my salary in half and want me to pay them back for the overpayments."

"What? How could they make such a mistake? That sounds impossible. Are they sure? They are trying to kick you out, no, worse than that. Just unbelievable! What a bad company!"

"Well I don't have much way to challenge it right now because I need the salary deposits into my bank account in order to pay my basic expenses like rent, food, car, and other bills. And I need to keep my health insurance."

She stared out the windows of the apartment. The rain had stopped and the sun was coming out. Our second floor view was a collage of red, brown, green, and yellow Fall leaves from the trees in the front yard.

"Look out there David, Fall is here and it is so wonderful. Even the oldest person sees the seasons change less than a hundred times. What is the difference between fifty or sixty times? More important is to enjoy it — not miss what's happening. Now we need to pay even closer attention. How many more times can you and I enjoy the beautiful color changing leaves in our life times?"

She seemed so sad … but she was bravely trying to comprehend what I had said. I bit my lip and prayed that she would not desert me.

"The easiest procedure is for me to file for bankruptcy because I can't really pay the credit card bills on the lower salary. I talked to an attorney who handles this and it is pretty straightforward in my situation. I don't really have much choice at the moment. I've already given him most of the information that he needs."

She appeared to be numbed by all the news. She sat quietly, a pensive angel on a troubled cloud.

Oddly, I was getting more relieved as we talked. All the stress that had been building inside of me was being let out, like a tea kettle when the water finally boils. She turned towards me. Her faint smile cheered me up even more.

"It seems to be nicer weather outside now. How about a walk somewhere? I think we both need some fresh air and I promise to go slowly so that you can keep up."

"Good, let's go." I welcomed the opportunity for a change of scenery. Hopefully, some cool air would stop the sweating and start to calm me down.

Shin stopped in the bathroom and I went to the bedroom to get a sweater. Then I heard what should not have surprised me. She was vomiting into the toilet. 'My God,' I thought, 'I'm killing her. Please God, get us through this day.' As she came out of the bathroom, she was wiping tears from her eyes.

"I'm fine," she said anticipating my question. I said nothing. My stomach was a knot of nerves. I held the railing walking down the stairs. This was my habit now because with my cancer medicines, my legs were sometimes pretty weak.

The rain had cleared up and the sun was now shining brightly in the cool Fall sky. It was stunningly beautiful with the colored leaves against the puffy white clouds. With everything else that was happening, I hadn't realized that it was Fall again. It seemed that it was Shin who had brought this wonderful season to me when she arrived.

Two blocks from the apartment, Cambridge Rindge and Latin High School was housed in four brick buildings next to a park, a tennis court, and a small soccer field.

In the middle of the complex was the city's public library, a century old stone building that looked like a castle. A group of students played baseball, others studied books, and a mother watched as her two toddlers kicked dry colored leaves into a pile.

"David, why don't we sit here for a while, you're sweating and breathing heavy again. Please calm down, relax a little bit."

"Shin, don't worry too much. I will figure this out."

I knew that she had no easy solutions to the problems of my disaster. Of course, I didn't expect that. 'What did I expect?' I asked myself. 'I have no idea. Just don't leave,' I prayed. She seemed to be crying in her heart, so we just sat there in silence for a couple of minutes.

Then she continued, "So that was your big worry — the financial disaster that you're in?"

"I guess. But it's all connected to the cancer because no consulting career means no way to catch up and pay bills later by having lots of clients next year. Also I have a confession. As you know, I'm not a big drinker but in the last two weeks I've been

117

drinking a lot. I know it is terrible, but I couldn't go to work and I didn't know what to do. I have no friends to talk to. I was so lonely. To make matters worse, I had to organize all the paper-work for the bankruptcy and avoid the phone calls from the credit card companies. I started to drink to forget my problems and think about a happy future — otherwise I couldn't do a thing. Deep down, I knew alcohol wouldn't help anything but ... I'm so sorry all about this, I won't do that again."

"I see." She was deliberate and thoughtful. We walked quietly around the park watching the kids play.

I thought back to the same time a year ago when I had invited her to come to see the 'Head of the Charles' regatta on the Charles River next to Harvard and MIT. This involves a competition among rowing teams from colleges around the country. It is well-known and Cambridge becomes a hub of tourists and activities. Back then I had plenty of money and no cancer. What a difference a year makes!

We were full of plans for the future as we toured many of the buildings in Harvard University. I still remember the book-filled smell of the magnificent library at the college that day, where life and hope sprang from every page of the thousands of famous texts. I wondered now why we have made so much progress in accumulating knowledge about the physical and biological world and still know so little about the deadly killer called cancer.

We sat on a park bench and watched the sun set behind the trees. "David, when I fly from Boston to Seoul, I usually have to change planes in San Francisco. I like to look down at the ground over the country when there are no clouds. What you learn is that everything is so small, nothing is big or overwhelming. Whether it is thousand-acre farms, the Rocky Mountains, or even the Golden Gate Bridge, the lesson from the plane is that nothing is too big of a problem to solve. Sometimes I feel that they are almost tiny toys. Everything is a manageable size. How about let's put things that way? Somehow, we have to look at this situation from an airplane."

I kept quiet in the face of her marvelous insight. Her brain worked in a much different way than mine, I thought. And I loved the way her insights unfolded. We all have different recipes for making chocolate cake but in her case, she had a totally different way of making it and maybe some secret ingredients as well. To me, her brain always seemed to produce results that were astonishing and delicious.

Her deep wisdom comforted me as the sun was setting in a pink sky. And then twilight. Everything seemed calming after the stress of the day's discussions.

She continued with newfound optimism.

"Let's worry about your health first. The side effects are so harsh on you now and the alcohol certainly did not help. After we fix your physical condition, we can deal with money later. There will always be some way to make that work out. A lot of people have encountered serious financial problems and come back to be great successes."

We walked back to the apartment holding hands. Surprisingly, a strong and silent confidence was crawling into my body from her hand. It seemed to give me peace and tranquility. 'Thank you God, for sending this lovely woman to me,' I thought.

In the kitchen, she cooked a wonderful dinner — Korean spicy chicken, peas and broccoli, and rice. She gave me a big smile, "We will have great Korean food every night here, so you don't have to take me out to a restaurant ever again."

It was the first real meal in the last five days so it tasted fantastic.

After dinner, drained of energy, we sat on the couch and listened to Mozart. She described the details of her daughter's wedding in Korea. I felt almost relaxed as we looked at the pictures of her beautiful daughter Ejin and her new husband. It seemed as if I was getting my own life back.

Then we watched 'You've Got Mail' to avoid more talk about the difficulties before us. At the end, I wiped some tears from my eyes. Shin was sleeping with her head on my shoulder.

After the movie, I walked Shin to the bedroom and went to brush my teeth. Five minutes later, she was sleeping peacefully in the bed, her face angelic in the soft light.

About midnight, I started to feel pressure in my chest. It was slow and gradual and tight. I had never had such a feeling before. It wasn't sharp or traveling to my arms and feet so it didn't seem life-threatening, but I didn't really know. 'Jesus Christ,' I thought, 'Shin finally arrives to save me and then I die of a sudden heart attack.' I recalled the printed discussions of the side effects of my cancer medications. They had warned about blood clots causing a heart attack.

I moved a chair by the bed and sat there watching Shin sleep. The tightness left but then it came back again. My brain began to worry. What if I had to go to the emergency room? Just like my first trip to the Pocono Medical Center. If I had ignored my symptoms then, I would definitely be in much worse shape. I shouldn't ignore my symptoms now either.

But would Shin know what to do?

I made a list of my prescriptions and information about my cancer condition. I included the health insurance information that hospitals usually ask about.

The tightness left and then it came again. It was like someone were reaching inside my chest and clenching their fist causing my muscles to go into temporary spasms. I was tired but I wanted to monitor my situation. So I sat in the chair next to the bed and tried to keep awake.

I hated to wake Shin, but nothing had gone right about my medical condition so far. Eventually, I figured that I would rather be safe than sorry.

"Shin, I have to tell you something else."

I put my hand on her arm.

"Oh David, what is wrong?"

She got up instantly, "You look so pale."

"Listen Shin, don't be scared. Right now, my chest feels funny and I'm staying awake to watch out for a heart attack. I don't really think it's that serious, but I do want you to know what to do in case it gets worse."

She sat up completely in the bed, with eyes wide open.

"Sure, I will take care of you. What should I do?"

"Just call 911 and tell them that you need an ambulance, give them this address, tell them possible heart attack, and answer any questions that they have. When the ambulance gets here, tell them to take me to Mount Auburn Hospital emergency room. That must be about three miles away. Here is a list of the medications that I am taking. They will probably ask about that. It also has Dr. Portinari's pager number on it in case they need to contact him."

"How will I know when it's an emergency and that I should call?"

"When I am grabbing at my chest and waving to you, that will be the sign. Also if I go unconscious. Hopefully, this whole thing is just a false alarm. But I think we need to be prepared just in case."

"How about heading to the hospital now rather than waiting for your chest tightness to get worse?"

"It doesn't seem that serious yet, but I will sit here next to the bed to monitor it."

My brain was aching with the disappointment and failure that I was bringing to her. Cancer, financial disaster, now a possible heart attack. When would I bring her happiness? When could we go back to life as carefree happy travelers?

Now that she was awake, we talked quietly in the early morning, waiting with anticipation for the next day to come.

"When you were gone, I was worried because I never volunteer or help other people. Basically, I'm pretty selfish."

"David, you're wrong about that. You are a great father for Dan and Amy and also a good husband for a long time. You took good care of your family and you are kind, appreciative, and supportive. And you know what, you didn't even call me when everything was falling apart — you didn't want to disturb me at the weddings. Most of all, you are a good human being. You are not a selfish person at all. Where is that piece of paper?"

She drew a circle on the back of my list of prescriptions. Then another one around the first circle. Finally, a third one which went around the other two.

"Please give me that yellow magic marker over on the dresser."

She colored in the innermost circle.

"My definition of selfish is based on this picture. This small circle in the middle is you, Dan and Amy and me too. You have to take care of those people first … especially yourself. I mean everybody must stand up on their own two feet. That's not selfish, that's sensible. The next circle includes your parents, close friends, and other people who you respect and know well or who need you. But only after you have the inner circle under control, can you go to the close friends circle.

"Finally, the third circle is for all the other people in the world who need help … these are people you don't know. Sure they need something, so whenever you have a chance to help them, don't refuse and do what you can do. But you don't have to worry about them until you have the two inner circles taken care of. You need to keep things in perspective when you worry about being selfish. You are a great person. I think God loves you so much. Please forget this selfish thing. I love you and I think you are wonderful. By the way, how does your chest feel?"

"I still feel tightness, but your words are so soothing. My dearest Shin, I love you. You are always so full of hope and encouragement. You have such a positive approach to life. I always learn great things from you. Thank you so much for that. I am fine so far, so don't worry."

It was early morning now and the daylight was coming in the back window. A sort of anxious content settled over us. We took pleasure from each other's company ... something we both had missed desperately for the last several months. Definitely me.

"Well, David why don't we call Dr. Portinari about your heart since this is already in the morning?"

"He should be around at about 8 am so we'll do it then. It's still too early to call."

She started to make some breakfast for us. "What kind of food would you like to have now?"

My hands were shaking and my chest pain hadn't gone away yet, so I wasn't hungry. We decided to wait until we heard what the doctor had to say.

We had rested a little during the night but not nearly enough. Now, the stress and tension seemed to suck the oxygen out of our lungs. We sat on the coach in the living room watching the clock on the mantel ticking slowly. Our stomachs were tied in knots.

At 8 am, I called Dr. Portinari. The paging operator put me right through.

"Doc, I've had this chest tightness off and on all night. It didn't seem serious enough to go to the emergency room, but it makes sense to check in with you."

He fired a bunch of questions at me. "Is it sharp? Does it move to your arms or legs? How much weight do you feel on your chest?"

He seemed satisfied with my answers. "It's a borderline case, but I think you should go over to the Brigham and Women's Hospital emergency room and get an EKG and a blood test just to be sure. I'll check in with you when you're there."

"Ok, Shin and I will head over there now. Talk to you later."

In retrospect, he did the safe thing. Probably no doctor would advise a patient complaining of chest pains to stay at home. Particularly since my medications create some risk of a heart attack anyway.

————

Brigham and Women's Hospital is right next to Dana Farber in the middle of Boston's teaching hospital district — Harvard Medical School and Children's Hospital are right down the block.

It only took Shin a half hour to get there even though it was the morning rush hour. She had spent many years driving in Seoul, probably the city with the most aggressive drivers in the world. She weaved in and out, back and forth, faster than any ambulance could have done through downtown Boston's morning traffic.

She dropped me off at the emergency room and parked in the Dana Farber lot. In the meantime, I had been ushered into a small room with a young medical assistant, a computer and two chairs. He interviewed me based on a script of questions that appeared on the screen.

Then they put me on a rolling hospital bed and wheeled me into an emergency stall across from the nurses' station. Another medical assistant put little sticky tabs on my chest and stomach. These connected with wires to the EKG machine, the standard way to monitor heart attacks.

"No problem here," he reported, after he looked at the paper coming out of the machine.

Shin and I breathed a huge sigh of relief. A nurse came by and stuck a needle in my left arm to draw blood. "We'll see if there's anything wrong here."

"Actually, I have Multiple Myeloma, so I don't expect a great report." I wasn't sure if she had gotten the complete story or not.

"Well," she smiled cheerfully, "you're still alive so your blood must be doing something right. We'll have a report in an hour."

Now that the danger seemed behind us, we were getting hungry and thirsty. After the blood tests were back, a doctor came by quickly and reported that there was no indication of a heart problem but they wanted to watch me for several hours anyway to make sure everything is normal.

"Can I get some food and water?"

"Actually, not yet. We're going to do a procedure where we shoot some dye into the blood in your system around your heart and do a CAT scan on you then. This kind of MRI might be helpful just to finalize our review. So nothing to eat or drink until that's over. You're in the queue right now so just relax."

I urged Shin to go to the Au Bon Pain in the hospital lobby to get some food, but she stayed instead and told me all kinds of stories to cheer me up.

It seemed like a waste of a day, but on the other hand it was a distraction to let all the new information from the day before sink in and help us to devise some plans to move forward.

We waited and waited. We started reading magazines from the emergency room waiting area, old editions of Time, Newsweek, and People Magazine. An article about elementary schools caught her eye.

She has always had a big interest in children's education in Korea and the United States, sometimes comparing the two countries and sometimes describing her experiences with her two daughters. They have both graduated from the best university in Korea, which was 80% male, so I listened attentively.

"I taught them arithmetic when they were only five and six years old. I did this while they were playing in the kitchen while I was cooking.

'Ejin, would you help me cut the apple in half please and give half to your sister? How much do you have? Right, one half.'

'Ehang, take another apple. Let's cut it for both of you and me too. Give your sister a piece and me a piece. How much do you have left? Right, one third.'

I even combined arithmetic with piano instruction to tell them about the number system based on 10.

'Ejin, play these piano exercises ten times.'
But I could tell that she was bored before she finished.

'Ejin, how many times have you played it so far? Right, seven. And who is 7's friend? Right, he is 3. So you are almost done!'

'Ehang, who is 9's friend? Right, he is 1. One more time and you can go and play with your origami papers.'

So before they went to elementary school they gained a good grasp of much of basic mathematics just by playing with me. I always used whatever tools I had available to make learning fun ... even boring piano lessons. I feel like I have a special gift from God for teaching and learning."

It's true that I have always been captivated by her teaching skills. I really wish that I had more time to learn Chinese, Japanese, and Korean from her. Maybe I should let cancer point me that way. I showed her an article about the growth of China's economy.

"I had a dream last week that I was a famous China expert. I had written a book, could speak a lot of Chinese, and was advising lots of companies what to do."

Her reaction was reassuring, "You could have done that — in fact, after we get rid of your cancer, you'll be able to do that. Don't worry, you'll have plenty of time to study and write about all of East Asia."

At that minute, a guy came to wheel me down to the CAT scan rooms.

"Ok, my darling, I'll be right back. Then we can get something to eat."

The MRI technician put some dye into a vein in my arm and slipped me into the CAT scan machine as he took the X-Rays.

"This may burn a little inside and you might experience a strange sensation, like going downhill on a roller coaster really fast. But the feeling will go away in a minute."

The procedure was over quickly without any strange feelings and I was back getting dressed in the emergency stall talking to Shin in less than a half hour.

The emergency room doctor came by and said the EKG was fine, the blood tests were fine, and the MRI was fine. I could go.

No evidence of a heart attack. Chest tightness, that was it. Probably a symptom of steroid withdrawal. I breathed a sigh of relief. At least one disaster had been avoided.

"Shin, take me to the Au Bon Pain." I was unsteady on my feet and my hands were shaking. Now that the heart attack episode was over, I felt like I was suffering from dehydration and lack of nourishment more than anything else.

I bought a bowl of chicken noodle soup and a sandwich with eggplant, tomatoes, and feta cheese on an Italian bread called

Foccacia. I drank a bottle of water while we were still in line to pay for the food. Shin got another one.

"David, slow down, you're eating way too fast," she said after we had found a table.

"Oh, Ok, I'll try."

But I was so hungry that I couldn't stop myself.

"Still too fast. Do twenty chews before you swallow."

It was a big table and there was another guy there reading a book. "She's right, you don't want to choke and die right here in the hospital lobby." He noticed Shin's Asian appearance and said 'Hello' in Chinese.

I responded, "Actually, she's from Korea, the languages are quite different, especially the written forms."

"I didn't know that. Is Korean easy to read and write?"

I put more food into my mouth.

"She has been teaching me and I think so. The alphabet is entirely phonetic and the symbols were constructed by a Korean King in 1444. They are pretty easy to memorize and pronounce. A lot easier than the picture-based icons in Chinese."

Shin smiled, proud of me as her prize student. I guess she was letting me talk in a futile attempt to slow down my eating so I wouldn't choke.

The guy started to ask a bunch more questions about the Korean language. Shin didn't feel like explaining to him so she didn't answer. I said apologetically, "Actually I'd love to talk more, but I have to eat right now." I lifted the water bottle to my mouth with two hands. I was still shaking.

Shin volunteered politely, "You have to excuse him, he has incurable cancer and he just came from a visit to the emergency room for a possible heart attack from the chemotherapy medicine. He loves to talk about languages but he hasn't eaten all day."

The guy almost fell off of his chair. "Cancer! I am so so sorry. I didn't mean to make the joke about dying in the hospital lobby before. I'm sorry." He turned back to his book in embarrassment.

His response caught me by surprise, "Please, no problem."

After he left, Shin said, "I'm sorry David that I told the guy about your cancer. I hope it doesn't bother you. I thought that he might think that you were crazy because you were eating so much so fast. Plus, your hands were shaking and your voice seemed nervous. So I felt that I should explain a little bit about you, so you didn't seem so weird."

"That's Ok with me Shin."

"The whole scene was actually quite funny with thin me not eating anything and overweight you eating as fast as possible."

I smiled, "That's just fine telling the guy about cancer. By the way, can we stop to get some Dunkin Donuts before we go home?" I was kidding by then and we both laughed.

As we drove back to the apartment, I thought about the guy at the table. Was this the way people would react when I told them about cancer? I was certainly used to the news by now. And Shin and my kids had known for the last five months too. I hadn't told anyone else, so the only difficulty I had to deal with so far is people who notice my puffy face and bloated stomach.

Both of these could be from too much fast food and too little exercise. But this guy was in a real panic. How did I want people to react? What should I say to make them feel relaxed after they know?

The apartment was a great comfort as we walked in. But we had been sitting all day. Shin needs body movement to feel good, so I suggested another walk. "The food gave me energy. How about a walk to the river again?"

She smiled, "Are you sure? Will you be Ok?"

I felt pretty good since we had clear and convincing evidence that we didn't really have to worry about me having a heart attack. It's amazing how the relative context makes other things, like career worries, seem small in comparison.

_____

Past the Sanders Hall cafeteria, past the Fogg Art Museum, past the side of Harvard Yard, past the old stone church, past a dozen student dormitories. We strolled quietly toward the water. The park by the river was alive with activity with students reading, athletes running, toddlers kicking leaves, and older people visiting with each other.

The sun was setting in a sky dotted with puffy clouds. Shin and I watched the pinkish colors spread across the horizon. It was the same scenic place, but it was so completely different than when I was alone. The complexity of the sky mirrored our lives now. With constant changes, vivid colors, sunset and sunrise, the white clouds reflect a different scene every instant.

If we had no challenges, no cancer, no financial difficulties, we would never know the richness of human struggles and emotions. If the sky were always blue and cloudless, we would miss an essential part of our life here on earth.

I felt good even though we didn't have all the answers to solve our problems. As long as we have hope and know the value of life, we will be fine. I tried not to think that I was dying of cancer. For the moment, I was comfortable. Maybe I was also celebrating my departure from the senseless alcohol-laden depression of the previous week. Never again.

We watched the sun set and started back to the apartment. The air was cool so Shin buttoned up her beautifully colored cloth coat from Korea. I snuggled close to her since all I had on was a thin blue sweater.

Walking by a courtyard near some dormitories some students had built a fire to cook a barbecue. The smells of burning mesquite and hickory immediately transported us back several years ago to the California desert where we had made such grand plans.

A sudden wind kicked up the leaves and brought reality back.

Shin turned toward me, "This may sound critical but it's not. I'm just trying to emphasize that your situation is not as desperate as you think."

"Go ahead, I always love to hear your ideas."

"I think you haven't had that many hard times in your life. You were so lucky until you got cancer. So you should appreciate that you had good times before — a lot of people don't even have that. So please don't be so frustrated or depressed … it won't help your condition at all."

Her voice was steady.

"I have had such a difficult time throughout much of my life so I do know what I should be grateful for. I know what it's like to survive cancer. I had a hysterectomy to get rid of ovarian cancer when I was thirty-eight years old. It's not the same as yours, but I survived. Who knows if I went to the doctor just a few months later I might not be here right now. Ever since that time I believe I have a bonus life which I must be thankful for. God gave me more time. Since then I have treated my days as even more precious and special than before. God certainly watches over me no matter where I am or what I do."

She continued, "Look at my mother's situation … she really had hard times. There she was in poverty-stricken Korea after the war where you had to pay to enter the schools. She firmly believed in education, in all of her children, and especially in me as the oldest."

"One rainy night, she was crying softly when there was no food for supper because my father was too sick to work. We sat on the yellow tile floor in the two rooms that we rented in a small house. My mother took me aside and hugged me so tight. I was thirteen at the time so it was a little awkward. But I'll never forget what she asked me in the dark. The words still echo in my heart. 'Shin, would you be willing to quit school and work for a while to make some money to pay the school fees for your brothers and younger sister?" I could feel the pain in my mother's hug. 'Sure, mom.' My mother just sobbed quietly and wouldn't let go of me. I started work at the textile mill the next day. I was only thirteen at the time and it didn't seem like that big a deal. I learned later that it did have a large impact on the way I grew up. I worked there until I got married when I was twenty-five. But look at the choices that my mother had to make back then — that's hard times. David, you can't imagine the hurt and poverty she suffered."

We both wiped our eyes as we watched a group of students head off to the pizza shop near Harvard Square. The evening grew cold as we hurried past a red brick church, an ice cream store, and the museum towards our comfortable apartment.

"As you know, I never continued any formal schooling after that. But look, I'm still here. Now I've accomplished a lot in my life. David, try to be thankful for the good skills that God gave to you. Then you can overcome the difficulties a whole lot easier. You can do it. I'm here to help."

She stopped and turned so that she was looking directly in my eyes, "I know what it's like to have no money. You don't really know that feeling. Don't worry so much."

I could feel her confidence and courage swallowing me up like a sudden turn around the corner into bright sunshine.

Shin gently took my hand firmly, "David, I am committed to you. I will not leave you." I smiled with content. My cancer had captured my Shin. 'Bittersweet', I thought to myself, 'but victorious'.

A New Home

Shin still had jet lag from her trip so she wasn't sleeping very well yet. For her, days seemed to be nights for at least a week after she arrived. She was always full of stories about late night TV shows that I had missed, especially silly infomercials. So for many mornings, I was awake and she was resting on the couch.

As I watched her breathing peacefully, I thought about my life since I met her. I wonder if she knows how happy she has made me. Even though she was sleeping, I was so glad to be with her. Her mere presence was powerful enough to chase away my loneliness and bring smiles to my heart.

That afternoon, we were back at the river again. The swirling black water churned past in a hurry to get somewhere quickly. The park bench by the Charles River was hard and cold. A cool breeze made us shiver. The clouds came and went in a gray sky. We kept warm by snuggling close together. But my heart-breaking task continued. Shin quietly asked,

"Tell me how the finances got to this point. I will be happy to help if there is anything I can do."

"Well a lot of factors contributed. The truth is I never wanted to tell you all about this — I was trying to solve all the problems before you knew. Then everything would be perfect when we eventually live together. Unfortunately, it didn't work out that way.

"I sent a lot of money to Dan, Amy, and their mother, every month ever since the divorce. As I ran low on funds, I took my money out of the retirement accounts early and the government took a large percentage in taxes. Add to that the newsletter business that I tried to start that didn't work out. And before I started with IEC, I was really unemployed for several years, just doing small projects that didn't make much money. When IEC recently cut my salary in half, that meant that I couldn't pay my bills and had to file for bankruptcy."

"You mean, you gave Dan, Amy, and their mother everything even your retirement money and you must pay extra taxes? And now you have to worry about how to deal with cancer. To me David, you certainly devoted your life to your family, that's for sure. I think that is really fine, no regrets for that right? Don't be too hard on yourself!"

The compliment was comforting but I continued my bad news story. "I always thought that I could do anything as far as my career was concerned. I earned a lot of money before the recession. Making a good salary was never a problem my whole life. And I loved my job ... it was fun to work. But in the United States, the industry I was working in was not so good for the last several years. Eventually things started to get better and I was developing a great marketing program at IEC until I learned about my cancer. I had a lot of confidence and everything was promising — I always knew how to do it!"

"Unfortunately, now it is clear that I can't continue my consulting career. Look at me. No one would hire me like this ... even though my brain is still pretty sharp. When I really start to think about this downfall, I'm incredibly frustrated and depressed."

She put her hand on mine, "Don't worry David, there are plenty of people called cancer survivors. You will be one of them too."

An athletic guy in his sixties ran by on the path next to the river. I thought, 'Could I really make it that long?'

"Shin, when you weren't here, I started to get so lonely. I don't really have any friends to talk to about cancer or life or anything really. Most of all I was panicking to tell you my financial situation. You and I have so many wishes for so many things. So I felt really depressed — the first time in my fifty-four years of life. I have never been in this position before."

I continued, "You know, I still wish that I could wake up from this horrible dream and go back to normal. It's still so hard to believe ... deadly cancer, no money, no career, and at the same time I want to live with you. How can I take care of you? I was almost crazy. I just didn't know what to do. I drank wine every day for the last several weeks. That was something I did trying to survive until you got here. Of course that didn't help anything. I'm so sorry for that. But now I feel much better. I know that I must find a way to get my confidence back. Because you are here, I think I can do it. Your strength, optimism, and hope make me believe that I can accomplish something."

The river seemed cold and gray. The strong current carried leaves and small branches to a new home somewhere downstream. Shin was pensive and decisive.

"How about this David. First of all, what we should do now is find a cheaper rural apartment as soon as possible, move there, then all you need is some groceries, and money to run the car. I'm going to cook at the house all the time — you need healthy home meals anyway — so we won't need a lot of money. In the meantime, you go to the office and I will be the driver. Considering your health condition, you will eventually be trying to change your job. I'm sure we can find something great for you."

She smiled confidently and continued.

"At the same time, we keep up the cancer medications and whatever Dr. Portinari tells you to do to keep your body healthy. Some days you feel physically miserable ... like today. Your hands are shaking, you look pale, you seem light-headed. Even when you have a puffy face it is Ok, we can take a walk, get exercise, have good food, wait a couple of days until you are able to work. Don't worry too much about other people and what they think about your appearance or if you are disoriented at work. A little bit later when you tell them about your cancer, they will all understand you and even try to help you."

"Shin I love you so much! I will do just what you said. I have all the confidence in the world that you and I together can fix most of these problems. The cancer cure we have to leave to the medical experts and God's hand. Other than that, we just have to stay focused and work hard. I know how to do that. This sounds like a great plan."

"It's more than a plan of words, David. An old Korean saying is, 'No more talk. Just do it'. The English idiom is 'saying is one thing, doing is another'. That's my philosophy. Besides, we don't have a choice."

We walked back to the apartment with lighter hearts. Two married graduate students walked by with a stroller. Their baby girl was about one year old and was smiling and playing with a plastic toy. Her mother and father were holding hands. We smiled and said hi.

It was clear that Shin was becoming the architect of our life together. And she was not afraid of cancer or lack of money. This angel of strength was amazing and inspiring. She was saving me from my misfortune with a compass that was both delicate and firm.

We woke up well-rested to greet a fantastic sunny Sunday morning. Since I slept a lot and Shin's cooking was giving me nourishment, I was so excited. Now I have a plan for success. No, I mean 'we' — We have a plan for success. I felt relaxed and rejuvenated, and my hands were less shaky too. We had coffee, juice, bananas and yogurt. I thought, 'this is great, maybe we should relax and enjoy life today'.

Shin walked into the living room after her morning shower. She bubbled, "How about a road trip to enjoy the Fall colors and in the meantime, find our new house today?"

"I'd love to do that except the part about 'find the new house'. Maybe we should wait for a week and see what happens before we try to move. I'd like to take it easy today and I want you to have a fun time after all the tension of the last few days."

She smiled at me but said, "No!" Her answer was clear.

"We have to act now. There is no time for moping around and considering alternatives. Especially when you feel good physically, we should do what we need to do. We will have fun looking at the leaves but we will also accomplish something as well."

There was no way to argue with her decision.

She said firmly, "Get your shoes on. Let's go."

I knew that the newspaper we wanted was the Metro West Daily News covering apartment rentals in the rural area around Route 495 to the west of Boston. We stopped at the news stands in Harvard Square to buy a copy. But they didn't carry it. I knew it would be at the grocery stores out in that area, so we headed west on Route 2.

We passed Walden Pond where Thoreau had spent several years in his famous cabin. Shin loved this place because it had a sense of history and a nice place to exercise as well.

"David, last year when you took me here I had a wonderful impression of Henry David Thoreau. That's what we need, a rustic cabin and a low-cost rural lifestyle like the great author had in his life."

"I do remember the last time we were here, before I had cancer. I actually ran about a third of the way around the pond. I had a lot of energy and was trying to impress you and convince you to live with me. And then you pulled me over to read the great author's quote on the sign near where his cabin used to be.

'I went to the woods because I wished to live deliberately, to front only the essential facts of life, and see if I could not learn what it had to teach, and not, when I came to die, discover that I had not lived.' "

I was proud that I had remembered this wonderful lesson on how to live.

Shin smiled, "How extraordinary — it seems to foreshadow our situation."

The way Shin deals with tasks is both adventurous and fearless. At the same time, she is smart, strong and sweet. Sitting next to her in the car I was just amazed. The sun momentarily blinded my eyes — I felt a thrill of delight just for a second or two. It was a genuine ray of happiness.

What a contrast with several weeks ago when I was alone with the poisonous cancer in my blood. I was terrified, tense and stuck hopeless in the most depressing period in my entire life. But now with Shin, I could do anything — just like a year ago.

We found a grocery store in Stow that carried the right newspaper. Shin studied the listings as I went to the Dunkin Donuts nearby to get us some coffee.

When I got back, she excitedly announced that she had found our new home. I was a little skeptical since house rentals were rare in our price range. We only really needed one bedroom, a fairly unusual size for a house. I studied the listing that she showed me.

'For rent, $1,000 per month, small one bedroom house on a pond in central Massachusetts. Available now."

I couldn't believe my eyes. This was perfect.

I called the phone number listed in the newspaper and talked to the owner of the house, Charles Dorby.

"We're very interested, when can we see it?"

"It's a nice vacation house on North Pond near the border between Milford and Upton. Go ahead and visit — when you get there, call me again and I will give you the code to unlock the door and let you in."

When we drove into the driveway, we knew it was ideal for us. About fifty yards down a gently sloping hill stood a small brown rustic cabin right next to the pond. The roof was pointed like a small Cape-style house and the sides were covered with dark brown shingles.

A granite plaque with a welcome pineapple hung next to the front door. The trees in the yard were aglow with the reds and browns and yellows of Fall in the sun. The reflections of the trees and clouds in the pond sparkled brilliantly. Hope and luck seemed to refresh us like a cool breeze on a hot summer day.

We both exclaimed, "This is it!" at the same time. We looked at each other with smiles of triumph and relief.

We called Charles again and got the code to open the front door. Once inside, we found a living room, study, and kitchen all facing the pond. There is a deck over the water and an enclosed porch for eating and talking when the weather is not so cold. The living room has a sofa bed where we could sleep.

A small upstairs has a bedroom with two beds and two closets. It seems like it would be too cold for sleeping up there in winter so we can use it for storage for clothes, photos, books, computer equipment, and important papers. There is even a rowboat that we can take out on the pond.

We both were smiling because we knew that this was a clear sign of hope and optimism. Ducks on the pond paddled by as a light breeze pushed the water South.

"Shin, this is the rural house we have been dreaming about, just perfect for you and me. I know you like to live a quiet rural life rather than in the busy crowds of the city. Plus it saves us money because it's only half the cost of the Harvard Square apartment."

"Yes, this is perfect ... especially, the parking situation. I always like to have my own parking space. Here we have our own driveway."

The next step was to call the owner and arrange to sign a lease, pay rent, and get the keys. But I was hesitant to call Charles again because it would interrupt his real estate meetings that day. This was a weird sensation. It seemed that cancer and the chemotherapy medicines had taken away my confidence in talking with the public.

But this house was just what we wanted and we needed to move quickly. And I didn't want to make any mistakes. Shin was already packing the things in the apartment in her mind. She insisted that I call Charles right away. It made sense so that's what I did.

"I'm sorry to interrupt your open house, but we would definitely like to rent the house. When can we sign a lease and give you the first month's rent?"

Charles seemed pleased to rent the house to us and he was a big fan of the Internet.

"Great, I will email you the lease and rental application. Then we can meet on Tuesday morning at the house, sign the lease, and you can give me the first and last month's rent plus the security deposit."

———

Later that night, I became worried about the paperwork that Charles had sent in the email. Most of it was standard rental contract documents. But the application form was from the Massachusetts association and it looked like it wanted a complete financial history.

I had owned a house for twenty-five years and the apartment in Cambridge was just a month-to-month rental for business executives. They didn't obtain the usual rental information. So I was unfamiliar and uncomfortable with the paperwork which seemed to be designed for newly married couples or kids just out of college.

I was worried that he might check my credit report and find that I owed a lot on my credit cards. I provided most of the information, but omitted my social security number so he couldn't check my credit rating. I hadn't missed any payments yet but the amount of the debt put me in a riskier category.

In my email to him, I said that I would give him a copy of my current credit report that I had obtained on the Internet. That still looked fine.

While I was emailing Charles, Shin was packing up our clothes into suitcases and the books into plastic bags from the grocery store. These turned out to be a fantastic idea. Rather than a heavy cardboard box of thirty books, she had assembled very manageable bags holding no more than a dozen. Much easier for me to carry in my condition.

On Tuesday morning it was raining.

I turned to Shin, "I wish it were sunny today. That would be good luck and would put Charles in a good mood so that he would rent to us."

"I like the rain better, you know why? Because it will definitely help us rent it. In the rain, the house doesn't look its best, so he will be even more anxious to complete the deal. Of course, you and I love the house no matter what."

What a brilliant observation. Of course she was right. Why did I have it just the opposite? And where did she get her precious way of looking at the positive side of things?

She had rescued me, found a new home, and helped arrange my finances. Next stop, we conquer cancer — bring it on, we are ready to fight.

We filled the car up with suitcases of clothes, books, laptop computers, and household goods. I had no furniture except three folding wooden bookcases. But since the new home had an assortment of tables, chairs, couches, and lamps we were all set.

When we got to the house, Charles gave us a complete tour before discussing the lease. It was built by his grandfather in the 1930's and expanded in the 1960's. Originally there was no heat so it was just used in the summer. Now there was hot water heat using oil so it could be kept warm all winter.

The house was so perfect for us that I was still nervous something would go wrong. I so desperately wanted to live there and start a search for my new career. Suddenly, Charles started signing the lease and we were done.

My heart quietly celebrated. Finally something had gone right. This was a big cut in expenses and was a wonderful place to live.

Charles asked, "When will you move in?"

"We already have suitcases and books in the car now. We will make a couple of trips today and sleep here tonight. I hope it's Ok with you, we should have everything moved in over the next few days."

"Sure, give me a call if you have any questions or need anything."

"Well, thank you" Shin said as she started sweeping leaves from the patio near the front door. Charles left and we hugged in happy celebration.

Maybe now my luck was turning. Just like Shin had assured, God was showing me a road for my life journey ... not impossible, just unfamiliar.

In order to save money, I also started canceling services that I didn't really need anymore. The health club in Cambridge, the parking garage, the T-mobile WI-FI wireless account, the Earthlink account, and the Netflix video rental service. It's surprising how much you can save when cancer and money are the major forces in your life.

On my list of things to do were to go by the apartment rental agency and tell them I was moving out and pay them for the last several weeks. There was no lease involved so it should be pretty straightforward.

But now I was so exhausted from things happening so fast, I needed time to rest. With my medical condition, my brain and body are just not used to such physical exertion and rapid changes. Even though Shin did a lot of work packing and moving, I had tried to help as much as I could. Plus, I had to make periodic appearances at the office to meet with the other consultants.

I leaned back in the car passenger seat and closed my eyes.

Shin was still full of energy. "Look, the rental agency is only four blocks from here and it is right on our way to our new home. Let's stop in and close the account now."

"Shin, I'm way too tired both mentally and physically. I could hardly make it into their office."

"David, it's only 4:30 so they are still open. You said you needed to talk to the manager. Why should we take an hour to drive back here later in the week to do something so simple?"

"Shin, I just can't, I feel dizzy and shaky. Maybe it's the medicines again."

"I strongly suggest that you listen to me … please. Just do it. No excuses. This is easy, compared to the other challenges ahead of you. It doesn't matter how you look now. Let me hold your hand"

We walked into the agency and told the manager that I needed to go to Dana Farber and get treated for a medical problem. We didn't mention any specifics but my appearance suggested something pretty serious. And most people in Boston know that Dana Farber means cancer anyway.

"We will be out by the following Monday ... "

Shin interrupted, "No, we will be gone by Friday, 5 pm. I've packed up almost everything already."

The clerk printed out an invoice and I wrote a check to close the account. The whole process took about ten minutes and was simple to finish.

I thought, 'Mission accomplished' as a great weight was lifted from my mental list of things to do. Shin had been right. And she's firm when it's time to take action. She really knows me.

On Friday afternoon, we sat on the couch in the empty apartment. The only thing left was the map of the world with China in the center. We had already taken the map of Europe and carefully rolled it up and put it in the car. I was exhausted and thought it was Ok to leave the China one. Besides, that dream was on hold for now. Shin agreed.

We took our last showers at the apartment not only to get rid of the sweat caused by all the moving activities, but also to try to wash away the tragedy that had stalked me since May. It was now 4 pm.

We sat on the couch to rest for the next step of our journey.

Looking at each other, it was clear that this was the end of an era. In a matter of days, Shin had helped me dramatically change my emotional state. She had taken me from a dark and bottomless terrifying hell to a land full of promise with her bright encouragement. Our humble cabin on the pond was full of hope and possibilities.

Now we were ready to address the new career, deal with bankruptcy, and fight cancer. With Shin as my compass, I was finished with miserable loneliness and negative outlooks and hopeless thinking.

We were heading for the next chapter of our lives, never looking back, holding hands together.

We were moving on.

Optimism and Two Edge Swords

After we had moved out of the apartment, driving to our new cabin on North Pond was the happiest moment since I learned that I had cancer. Something inside made me feel so thankful to God for this new beginning.

The next morning, we couldn't believe our eyes it was so beautiful. The sun sparkled on the water and reflected into the many windows of our new home. Looking out, we could see the reds and yellows and browns of the trees on the other side of the pond. The magnificent forces of nature seemed to be bringing us a powerful and magic optimism. It was far more than I could have ever imagined.

"Shin, you don't know how happy I am now, and how much I appreciate you. You are right — God must have sent us to each other. From now on I will do anything for you like you did for me. Look at me, my hands are not shaking any more and I'm not afraid of my cancer either. Compared to a month ago, I am a totally different person mentally and physically. I love you deeply and thank you again for being here."

"David, I love you too. Just be positive, I will try my best to take care of you. We still have a lot of things to get done together."

She had made our bed in the Korean style in the living room on the floor. Layers of a green sheet, a sleeping bag, a yellowish quilt with red roses, then another burgundy quilt with dark red flowers and stripes and four pillows.

146

"The mattress in the sofa bed is too soft. I'm not so used to that. Plus a firmer bed is better for your condition anyway. You will sleep much better on the floor."

Somehow, the new bed made me feel strangely safe and relaxed. To me, she always knows what she is doing … everything that she touches becomes full of a special magic.

Shin made fresh ground coffee and we then had some fruit with orange juice. She also cooked hot plain rice, which I eat with milk and honey. She eats her rice with spicy cabbage called *kimchi* and a side dish of dried anchovies with honey.

"David from now on we are going to have a healthy Korean food diet. It is mostly the same ingredients as in America but much less oil, more vegetables, less fat, and more spice and garlic. This will help you cut your cholesterol and your weight and may even help out with your cancer. Plus it's going to be delicious, believe me."

Then she unpacked the books into the floor-to-ceiling bookshelves on the left side of our living room. I spent most of the time sitting in the armchair with white cushions since I was still really short of energy.

My mind reeled when I thought about the speed of events since she had arrived. It is absolutely unbelievable to me that we had completely rearranged our lives in a week — including a hasty move from our Cambridge apartment to our new cabin on North Pond. It certainly reflects the efficiency, speed, focus and most of all, love that Shin has brought to my life.

A feeling of peace and resolution descended over me as I watched her. I began to accept life, death, money, and even cancer. I felt that Shin had restored my will to move forward with her strength and confidence.

She sensed my comfort and that made her happy, "Everything is under control, we are settled down and ready to fight cancer together. In the meantime, we will enjoy each day as a precious gift."

After lunch, Shin kidnapped me and drove me on a trip around our pond. We found Sandy Island Beach on a small peninsula on the other side. There was a little park with grass and trees and a swing set. It was deserted now but probably quite crowded in the summer. Red, brown, green, and yellow leaves coated the ground and reminded me of when we would make piles to jump in when I was young.

The sand area stretched several hundred yards along the shore. The water is so clean I had heard that the town gives swimming lessons here during the summer.

I said to her. "Look across the pond, we can see our house from here."

I guess I was surprised that it was so near.

"I knew that, that's why I brought you here. To get a different perspective on our lives and the house too. Many times, that helps deal with the kinds of changes we are going through."

"Shin, I remember the first time when we met. We started talking on the tour bus around Tokyo. You showed me how to read Japanese characters as we admired famous temples and attended a formal tea ceremony and visited Tokyo's major shopping areas. I thought you were a genius ... a college professor or something like that. Plus you were so pretty and young-looking and energetic. And you exhibited a quiet wisdom when you talked about people and life. I fell in love with the the fist time that we met. Thinking back to that warm summer day in Tokyo, it is still hard to believe that you are here with me now!"

"You know what? You're right. As you said, what has happened to us ever since we met is almost unbelievable. David, do you know what your favorite sentence to say is? 'This is good, this is good' … you always say that. That is what makes me love you and help you. When I see you smiling and joking and laughing, my heart is so full of joy. Besides, you always listen to me and respect me and believe in my ability to accomplish new things. When my daughters first left for college, I felt depressed so much of the time even though I have a lot of friends and activities. I didn't know how to be happy. Now when I'm with you, I'm not lonely any more."

We walked in the sand along the water several hundred yards around the beach. Small waves made a steady plop as they settled on the shore. I had always been amazed at the instant compatibility between us. We are always talking to each other about everything, people, nature, movies, books, past events, future plans, whatever. We have so much to give to each other. I've never had this kind of feeling and relationship before.

"When you have to go to Korea to visit the girls, I miss you so much. I am sick with worry and doubt. When you arrive back to me, it is like a ray of sunshine through my whole body. But I know it is important to see your daughters so I know that you must go sometimes."

"You know what, David? Let me tell you one strange situation in Korea. When a woman marries the oldest son of the family, that young couple must have a boy — at least one, so the family blood continues down to future generations. I was in that position but I had only two girls. When I gave birth to my younger daughter it was so weird because nobody was smiling at my baby, although she was so beautiful. Then three weeks later I realized that they were all hoping for a boy. The same night, I declared to my husband and the family that I'm not going to have any more babies. If I had a boy after my two girls, everybody would love the boy more than my girls — perhaps even me because I inherited the feeling from my mother. But now God gave me these two precious daughters to take care of until they can stand on their own two feet. I am going to raise them the best I can. I love my children so much. I also know that when they are grown up I must let them go. Now Ejin is married and my younger daughter Ehang has a boyfriend at the bank where she works. So she will leave me soon too. Then I really will be free."

I picked up a small flat gray stone from the shore to try to skip it on the water in the pond. I remember showing my kids how to do it many years ago. I gave it a try — it skipped three times!

"Shin, it seems like only yesterday my twenty-eight year old son Dan was born. He was premature ... three months early, he was so small. But the moment I saw him I loved him so much — he was just marvelous, so special. As time went by, Dan's mother and I realized that he needed much more attention from us then a normal child. So through all that time, 'Stay with him, be there for him' was my life motto. Although he is twenty-eight now, many of his interests are not so complicated at all. He graduated from a two year college with help from a tutor, and after we got divorced, I visited him several times a week. After that, he learned how to do things on his own so he has been much more independent. Now he works at the library, and volunteers at the hospital and a local food bank. After I learned about my cancer, I started going to see him once a week to play video games and eat lunch and talk. Sometimes we check his computer for viruses or fix various software programs that he uses. He is always smiling and happy and pure. His understanding of life is less complicated and more straightforward than ours. His approach has helped me a lot over the years. Now with cancer, I have to learn even more from him about the simplicity of life."

On the ground we found a fluorescent pink tennis ball. We threw it back and forth playing like kids while I continued to talk.

"I do remember one time when I did a lot of work to help Dan out. In middle school, he had acquired a serious stutter which happened at both home and school and out at stores. It was so bad that sometimes he couldn't even talk. We discussed this with several speech experts at school but they couldn't help. It was so frustrating. To make matters worse, there were five kids at school who had taken the habit of mimicking Dan's problem and teasing him about it. When Dan mentioned this on a walk one day, I couldn't help but cry later. How could I help fix this? I loved him so much. First, I wrote all the parents of the five kids and told them to tell the kids to stop. They did and that helped a little. Next, I spent several weeks searching and calling to find a speech expert who specialized in stuttering. I found a program run by Sophie Jacobson at the New England Rehabilitation Hospital in Woburn. She had just the right program every morning for a small group of kids for six weeks in the summer. There was practice each evening as well. That cured the problem. She knew exactly what she was doing and we completed the homework religiously."

"Has the stuttering ever come back?"

"Not at all. Plus he has some tricks to do in case it does. We still have all the books with the exercises. It makes me so happy to know that I helped improve Dan's life. When he got to high school, he had a much happier experience."

Shin stopped and hugged me. "You are such a good father! Kids are really amazing, aren't they? I used to say that whoever has no children, knows only one part of love."

"Yes Shin, but most of all when I think of love, it is you sticking with me, cancer, no money, and an emotional roller coaster. You are so precious and wonderful. I know that you love me because of what you're doing."

When we got home from the beach, it was dark. Shin ran down the hill to our house from the driveway.

She is always the first one in the house since I take it slower because my legs don't work as fast as they once did. She turns on the heat and lights for me so I can see where I am going. One cute thing that she does when she gets to the house first is to remove the shades on all of the lamps. As a furnished rustic cabin, the lamps look like a collection from a rummage sale. Several of them had delicate shades that simply hooked onto the light bulb using a wire frame.

Shin removes them to get more light — she loves to have a bright room. In contrast, I attempt to make the room cozier by putting the shades back on. To me, a bare light bulb is more like a prison. So we have a polite agreement to disagree and are constantly putting the shades off and on depending on whose feelings are stronger at the time.

When I got there, I put the shade on really quickly on a lamp in the study. The room looked warmer and more inviting that way. Later that night, when we were watching TV in the other room, Shin said,

"What's that funny smell? I don't have anything cooking. But it doesn't smell like food anyway, more like burning plastic."

I jumped up and ran into the study.

Sure enough, I had not put the shade on correctly and it rested directly on the light bulb. It was half-melted and was ready to start on fire. Shin had followed me into the room.

"David, I told you not to put the shade on," she smiled widely.

"But do you still love me now Shin?"

"Yes my dearest. I couldn't be happier than when I am with you. God put us together because he knew we needed each other."

We settled into a routine of weekly activities that took my cancer into account. Some days, when the side effects from the medications were minimal and I looked pretty good, Shin would drop me at my IEC office in Harvard Square. Then she would shop around Cambridge and the Prudential Center in Boston. Before she picked me up in the late afternoon, she would stop at the Korean grocery store to pick up some special foods.

When I was working on projects that could easily be done without meeting other consultants, I worked at home on the computer. This could handle days when my side effects made my appearance a little rough for a visit to the office. I felt that I would get too many questions and second looks. Much better to avoid IEC on those days ... I still had not told anybody at work about my deadly cancer.

Sometimes when I stayed at the house, Shin would head downtown Milford to the Midtown Women's Fitness Center, a health club that she had joined to get exercise, use the sauna, and take a shower.

Sometimes I would go with her and work at the Milford Public Library, less than a block away from where Shin was. There, I could plug in my computer, do Internet research, and browse the shelves of wonderful books. It wasn't fancy like the nice oak historical reading rooms of the libraries at Harvard, but the books still opened up vast new worlds of thinking and entertainment.

Life had settled into a peaceful pattern. I seemed to be adjusting better to my chemotherapy drugs — in any event, I had Shin to take care of me if I really had a bad day.

One Sunday morning, I woke up at dawn. Shin was still sleeping peacefully so I quietly went onto the porch. I sat in a comfortable wicker chair with faded multi-colored cushions.

The pond was covered with fog. I couldn't even see the water thirty yards away. The trees on the shore near the house were stark against the white mist of nothingness.

After a half hour, the fog lightened ever so slightly so that I could see a very dim view of the white house across the pond. This is like my future, I thought. Sometimes I can only see for thirty yards. Other times the fog gives me a brief taste of months to come but nothing firm, just very hazy outlines. I don't really have the clear days that other people do.

At one point, the fog showed the white house across the pond dimly. But then to the left, I could make out the outline of a large brown house through the trees.

How could this be? That house doesn't exist.

But it sure seemed real. Maybe that is where I will go when I'm finished in this world. That would be ideal because there is a clear view into the many windows of our house from across the pond. I could easily keep an eye on Shin … is she in the kitchen cooking rice soup or spicy chicken? Is she at the computer using the Internet to read Korean newspapers and magazines? Or is she in the living room watching Lifetime channel shows or CNN Headline News? Is she on the porch doing exercises?

Is she smiling or is she crying?

Oh how I wish this were not happening to me!

I walked outside to clear my head. Five swans paddled by heading North. I always wonder where they sleep.

———

When I went inside, Shin was cooking rice. For breakfast, Koreans generally eat the same things as for lunch and dinner. Cold breakfast cereal is rare and donuts are still snacks for kids for after school and after dinner. I'm still trying to get used to this but she encourages me to have low calorie food for most breakfasts.

So my morning foods include many different choices now — steamed yams with margarine and little bit of cinnamon, plain low fat yogurt with bananas, hot rice soup with carrots in it, and of course regular American food like cold cereals.

Then lunch and dinners are even healthier. She creates dishes to make sure that I get enough vitamins and low cholesterol and calories. She also uses a large amount of garlic which is very healthy. The way she cooks it, there are no strong smells and it tastes excellent. Now I am a big fan of garlic ... and some say it may even help fight cancer.

One of my favorite Korean recipes is *tak kalbi*, cut-up chicken cooked with spicy red bean paste sauce, green peppers, onions, garlic, ginger powder, and a little honey. When served with rice this is absolutely fantastic. And low calorie too because she cooks the chicken in water ahead of time to remove the fat.

One Sunday, when both the library and the health club were closed, I persuaded Shin to drop me at the Barnes & Noble bookstore at a busy shopping center in Bellingham to browse and read. The shopping center also has a Staples store with computer parts and software for me, and a Wal*Mart and a Market Basket grocery store for Shin. I didn't feel so bad spending time at the bookstore because she could shop at the other stores when she was tired of the books.

The shopping center is about a half hour drive from the house. As usual, we talked as we drove there.

"Shin, I've always had a pretty content and optimistic life, so I have never really had to deal with depression and feelings of hopelessness. Now cancer has changed all that. And the money problems complicated that as you saw. My depression really made me feel like I had hit rock bottom. But now I have hope again. Thanks to you, I think I'm starting to understand the true meaning of the word 'optimistic'."

I continued, "You have motivated me to finish some important tasks quickly but then to adjust to the slower lifestyle of a cancer patient. I am starting to think about myself as a 'cancer survivor'. It is hard because there are still many steps to take before it actually happens. I still carry the coffee that I buy at Dunkin Donuts with two hands to take a drink.

And I always hold the railing when I walk down stairs. The other side effects make life miserable on some days. At first, it was always much easier to take one day at a time, without planning the future.

But now, visions of life a year from now sneak into my brain sometimes. Before, I used to push such thoughts away immediately. Now I enjoy them. That's hope for me. I want to be a cancer survivor and change my career and organize my money so I can play and talk with you. And take care of you just like you take care of me."

"That's a great new attitude. As you know, David, I have a lot of goals for the future. I always want to learn and do new things. I need to fulfill my dreams to go new places and to expose myself to new experiences. I need to catch up on the education that I missed at school, and continue to expand on that all the time. I was so lucky to get where I am now. Look, already I've learned English almost ninety percent and I've traveled quite a bit around the world after the girls were grown up and in college."

She put her hand on my leg as she frequently does when we are driving together.

"David, do you remember a book I read recently, 'Adventure Capitalist' by Jim Rogers? That was my plan. Driving in many countries around the world meeting people, seeing new things, and tasting exotic foods. I probably would be doing that if I were not staying here. Of course, now my biggest challenge is to care for you and get rid of the cancer so that you and I can travel around the world and keep going until our life journey is over."

I smiled, "You can still travel around the world ... just wait until I'm gone."

Ignoring my attempt at humor, she continued, "You are the first person to really take an interest in making my dreams come true — I know that I can accomplish anything when I am with you. You are such a good and patient teacher. We should continue to teach and learn from each other, to play and talk, and also help each other as long as God gives us the opportunity to stay on this Earth."

I think that one of the things that made Shin like me is that I always treated her as an equal. This is quite different from the male-centric world of her generation in Korea. When she talks about life and feelings, I try hard to listen intently and respond and question. I seem to be giving her desperately needed attention that she has been thirsting for ever since her girls went off to college years ago.

But she certainly has an independent strength separate and distinct from me. I am always reminded of that when I watch her persistent and unwavering focus to learn the details and nuances of the English language.

She listens to CNN Headline News constantly as well as books on CD whenever she drives somewhere. I gave her several Pulitzer Prize winning audio books for Christmas once and she listened over and over — asking me for definitions and explanations as we drove.

One of her all-time favorites was 'Angela's Ashes' by Frank McCourt. She loves to recite parts of that book as we drive along. I feel close to young Frankie as he grew up with his family in the poor Catholic neighborhoods of Ireland … even though I have never read the book.

We pulled into the shopping center in a light drizzle. The Barnes & Noble bookstore was medium size but it had everything I needed — a coffee area to work on the computer, bathrooms, plenty of specialty magazines, and more books than I could read in a hundred lifetimes.

Before my financial disaster, I always felt bad if I didn't buy a book after I had browsed for a couple of hours. And I made numerous purchases at Amazon because it was so easy to find specialty books not carried in the stores. This strange addiction undoubtedly contributed to my large collection of books at home and the office. Now I had to dramatically cut back on my purchases ... but I still liked to browse for a long time.

"Look Shin, a book of Dave Barry humor columns."

I was laughing before I even picked up the book that I already had at home. His criticisms and exaggerations of real life events always made me smile.

"David, as you know, I'm not so interested in goofy books like that. I mean, I don't have time for that. I have to read books to learn, not to have fun. So now, I'm much more interested in real life stories, especially those about people who start with nothing, have lots of difficulties, and finally become a success."

She continued quietly.

"Not only money success but accomplish something special in their lifetime here on earth. A saint like Mother Theresa or a famous scientist like Marie Curie or Helen Keller and her teacher. I believe this kind of spirit keeps the earth spinning the right way. And it helps teach me how to live. Sometimes they remind me of what I have been through all my life time — it wasn't easy at all but now I feel that I have accomplished a lot. And I'm still not finished yet."

I tickled her stomach, "But how does such a happy, smiling person like you stay that way? Let me read you this funny story."

She gently took the Dave Barry book from my hand and put it back on the shelf.

"You know that I like to laugh but I probably will stick to the more realistic books. I don't mind when you read silly things, but I want to spend my time learning more about real people's stories until my life journey is over. TV shows and movies are the same thing, you like to watch Seinfeld and other goofy programs, but not me. I would rather watch stories which give me some thoughts, that is why I like the Lifetime channel and the other serious movie channels."

Actually, I enjoyed all kinds of books, both happy and sad, serious and silly. I still remember my first trip to a library when I was a kid. It was a white house that had been converted to hold several thousand books in a relatively poor town. Now I surveyed the shelves and shelves of print at Barnes & Noble — a limitless expanse of knowledge and emotions and information. To me this collection of human experience represented a wealth of opportunities for mental journeys across time and throughout the world.

Shin interrupted my thoughts, "By the way, how much longer will you be at the bookstore?"

"I have to check for a couple more books, then I'm going to work on the computer in the coffee area for about an hour. Is that Ok?"

"Sure, but I'm going shopping at the other stores and then down to the grocery store to pick up some things that we need. I'll meet you back here later."

Books to me are certainly a window into the world of humanity. But I rarely read a whole book. My habit has been to browse to get a flavor of what's going on, then stop, and quickly pick up another one, for another hit of sensation.

It's as if I can't quite make up my mind and focus long enough. Or perhaps it is the best way to sample a mass of information in our limited lifetime … languages, science, computer technology, the classics, new fiction, biographies of famous peo-ple, business exposés, and even self-help books.

Now I check for books about cancer and Eastern religions too.

When Shin came to get me an hour later, she had a big smile on her face.

"David, I got a great bargain at the grocery store. You need to drink a lot of liquids with your medications, right?"

"Yes, I have been pretty good about that, but still not enough."

"Remember the other time when I bought five bottles of sparking water to try to give you a variety of drinks? It tasted really weird and you said it's not just sparking water, it was tonic water. I never drink alcohol so I didn't even know what a 'gin and tonic' was. You were so sweet, to tell me 'don't worry I'll drink it all,' and it turned out that the tonic water helps control the cramps in your hands that are caused by the medications. You know how much I've got this time? I just bought one big box of tonic water. That is twenty-four one liter bottles. It was on sale!"

"Shin, you're so funny. It is good economically so what the heck, but we need to call a porter from the airport to bring that box from the driveway to the house — right?"

When we got home, it took almost a half hour to carry all the groceries including the box of tonic water down the hill. Shin unpacked and poured me a nice glass of sparkling water and one for herself too. Please enjoy your glass of tonic!"

She pursed her lips in shock at the bitter taste.

We both burst out laughing.

"At least it was really cheap on sale."

"My darling, you are the most wonderful shopper in the world and I love you so much."

I was so happy to have an almost normal life again. Shin had brought me laughter, happiness, and hope.

This was heaven.

One day, we both woke up early. The good thing about this house is that every morning at sunrise, it shines into all the windows and covers us with warm optimistic feelings. Shin asked me if I needed to go to the office, and mentioned that today is a good day because I looked pretty good — the puffy face and unsteady walk seemed to be totally gone for the moment. I could talk to some of the other consultants and Shin could shop and pick up some things at the Korean grocery store.

From our new house to my office in Harvard Square, the trip takes about an hour because there is always heavy commuting traffic. As usual, we talked non-stop during the trip.

"Shin, remember when I took you to see Dante's burial place in Ravenna when we were in Italy? He was a famous writer in the late 1300's who wrote a fantastic religious and philosophy book about hell, purgatory, and heaven all controlled by an elaborate adventure story. It's called the 'Divine Comedy,' but it's not really a humorous story, just the name has stuck in the translation from Italian."

"You studied Italian in college, right?"

"Yeah, that's where I first read this book. The big thing to me is the appearance of Beatrice, the woman he loves, to save him and take him through the heavens into Paradise to see God. Ever since I read that book, I have been searching for my Beatrice. Now I know, I am looking at her."

She smiled, her confidence showing in her sparkling eyes, "David, tell me more. What else happens in the story?"

"Dante starts his journey when he is lost in the woods and a famous Roman poet named Virgil comes to escort him through hell and purgatory to meet Beatrice who takes him to heaven. There is a lot of Catholic religious philosophy in there too. But at the same time, Dante makes it into a story about an exciting adventure. Along the way, they see and talk to all kinds of real people from Florence of the time who are in hell and purgatory. We find out what their sins were and how much they are suffering. At the same time, he meets all kinds of dangers like wild animals and cliffs to climb and rivers to cross while he travels the complicated levels of each territory."

"Eventually, he overcomes all the difficulties and meets the beautiful Beatrice in a rainfall of lilies thrown by angels. She takes him to paradise and to a vision of God. To me, it is a great story of rescue from difficulties and redemption from past mistakes."

"Wow, I should read that book some time. But my approach to God and religion is much simpler. As human beings, we think we know a lot but we don't." Shin continued with quiet confidence, "We can't predict what will happen in the future, we don't know when we will die. Young, old, alpha, omega, all these things we don't control. They are up to God. As hard as we try, we'll never know God's plan for us. But we do have love, trust, happiness, and hope. God gives us the wisdom to develop those and become a real person. Our job on earth is to do that successfully. We should thank God for giving us the strength and endurance to accomplish that."

We paid the toll and exited the Mass Pike at Cambridge. Over the bridge, down tree-lined Memorial Drive next to the Charles River, around the Kennedy School of Government, and over to my office. Shin dropped me off next to the Charles Hotel and we arranged to meet at 4 in the afternoon. I had a really good feeling about the day.

––––––––––

While I was at the office, a stroke of luck helped accelerate my career change plans. It wasn't great, but at least it was something. I got a call from the Cancer Survivor Center in New York City.

They had gotten my name from a nurse at Brigham and Women's Hospital. She had been impressed by my thirty second description of Multiple Myeloma — it had been medically accurate but perfect for the layperson to grasp quickly. I think I even had some humor in the explanation as well. That's the style that had gotten me on CNN and NPR so much in my past career.

Anyway, they have a big need for experienced speakers who could address large groups around the country. Most of them are interested in the challenges that occurred, both physically and emotionally, and the process used to overcome them to become a successful survivor.

They want real life experiences and will pay two thousand dollars a speech plus any transportation cost to wherever the group was located. I agreed immediately since I needed the cash to pay bills. The first speech is in New York City in a month.

The nice thing about the speaking career was that showing up with side effects would be fine since part of my qualifications is that I have cancer. So no problem there. And my research to develop and prepare the speeches could be done on days when I felt good. I could focus on my body the other days.

Plus, Shin could travel with me since she loves to see new places and meet new people. Overall, the speaking program would be a nice way to make some money to pay bills and contribute what I could to our understanding of the emotional roller coaster that cancer imposes on people.

"Guess what," I proclaimed excitedly as Shin picked me up.

"I just got hired to give a speech in New York to a group interested in the experiences of cancer survivors. They will pay me a nice fee to describe the challenges and how I overcame them."

"That's fantastic, you've given hundreds of speeches in your old career so you have a lot of practice. Actually, when you first found out that you had cancer at the Pocono Medical Center, you were there to give a speech. What was the name of that conference place, anyway?"

There was no way to forget.

"The SkyTop Lodge, a nice luxury hotel. But I never stayed there overnight — the conference director still jokes that I had a much more expensive hotel that weekend."

"Will this cancer survivor speech career continue or is it limited to just one speech?"

"Well, from what they say, they have requests from groups around the country who would like to hear speakers like me. They need people with humor, experience, and the ability to summarize the medical details for a lay person. I can easily do that — but I will have to do some research on other kinds of cancer and interview other cancer survivors to get more information. There should be at least three speeches a month. That will pay the bills. After that, we can see how much energy I have left."

On the drive back home, I celebrated my good fortune.

"Shin, I am the happiest man in the world — even with all of the challenges ahead. What a fantastic opportunity! And you can come everywhere with me when I give the speeches. This is good. This is good."

"David I'm so happy too … it looks like your change of career is starting to happen."

———

That night, after Shin had settled comfortably in bed, I went out on the deck to watch the almost-full moon on the water. A strong wind was pushing the waves relentlessly from the North. Whitecaps flickered in the moonlight.

I fervently respected the power of the water. It had always made me think about past, current, and the future in different ways. There seemed to be a special magical oxygen that I could breathe that caused my brain to function just a few degrees differently. Many of my most favorite memories are associated with rivers and ponds and lakes and oceans.

I took stock of my medical condition as I watched the waves. On my most recent visit to Dana Farber, the doctor had reported that the IgG measure of the cancer in my blood was good ... it had continued to go down using Thalidomide and Dexamethasone.

In several months I should have a stem cell transplant, which in my case is relatively safe and straightforward. A month hospital stay and another couple of months recuperation period, with lots of fatigue but with fairly predictable results. It is likely that it will put my Multiple Myeloma cancer into remission for maybe a couple of years. Then I can continue life at a slower pace for awhile with periodic checkups.

But I'm sure that life will not be normal. While I'm alive, I will be a 'cancer survivor.' Everything about people and nature will be different. The threat of really dying soon has caused me to learn and change so much. I think that I will be a better person after having gone through this. But most important is that Shin is with me now. And we know that we belong together.

The angst that I had about not being a better person now seems to be resolved. I would take better care of Shin and Dan and Amy, and try to thank all the people who helped me extend my life. I definitely will try to figure out a way to help others more.

The map of Europe is still rolled up next to the bookcase. Soon we will hang it on the wall. We have a lot of things to get done now, but Europe is definitely in our plans.

With Shin, anything is possible. What a difference she has made in my life! I am dying of cancer, have lost my professional career, and am going bankrupt, yet I am the happiest man in the world.

A cold wind blew by as I stood on the porch watching the pond. I shivered. Something clicked in my brain. Somehow, I knew these feelings of success couldn't last. They certainly didn't sweep all my problems under the rug. I have a lot of work and challenges ahead. Actually, my health is not good ... cancer will take my life, I know that. I will not live very many more years. Suddenly, my mind was full of pessimism.

The stem cell transplant hospital stay to control my cancer won't be pleasant — they actually kill all the blood cells and bone marrow in your body. Plus my money situation really is a disaster. The bankruptcy won't be easy ... and after it shows up in my credit report, it will be harder to reserve a hotel, buy an airplane ticker, or rent an apartment. Soon I will have to resign from my job at IEC because my health is so bad. Then I'll be unemployed making things much worse. Despite the optimistic talk, the cancer speaker job is still pretty tentative. Plus, I don't have a real plan to help take care of Shin when I'm gone. And I had no doubt that my chemotherapy medicine would cause my brain and body to go crazy again. I really am on a physical and emotional roller coaster that never stops.

The pleasant thoughts of progress and success might just be a case of foolish confidence. Everyone knows that what goes up must come down. I usually get into trouble when I forget that about cancer and hide from the reality of the situation.

For optimism is a two-edged sword. What follows it is always a frightening trip into the swirling, devastating waters of the Perfect Storm. So far, I return to the docks with the fish and a smile.

But some day, I won't come back. I know that, Shin knows that, and it is terrifying to us both.

The Christmas Messiah

Snow came early in November, large flakes drifting over the trees and disappearing into the wind-whipped water of the pond out our windows. Some mornings ice would start to form and then melt as the sun took over. The white snow seemed to bring a cold sadness and melancholy as it coated the pine trees with beautiful almost sterile postcard scenes.

Days came and left and the weather got colder as I waited for the doctors to decide the right time to do my stem cell transplant. The cancer medicine continued to slow me down and frustrate the activities that I had become accustomed to over the last thirty years. 'One day at a time', people would say. But where was the accomplishment in that?

The weeks were punctuated with periods of mild depression during times of steroid withdrawal. White birds circled the water going places in a hurry and the ducks avoided the ice in the pond as they paddled by searching for food. The trees across the pond had transformed from the bright colors of Fall to a dull brown and gray with streaks of dark green where the pine trees were.

All of a sudden, one morning the pond was frozen solid and ice fisherman dotted the horizon hoping to catch some bass or trout for dinner. A few days later, snow coated the ice and cross country skiers and snowmobiles joined the picture that we could see from our windows. I was getting weaker and could not venture out much but Shin would give me reports from her various walks.

Doctor Portinari was still waiting for the measure of bad proteins in my blood, the IgG, to go down to the right level before we could start the stem cell transplant procedures. But during the

167

wait, my fatigue level continued to increase … most likely due to the Thal-Dex medications.

At the same time, I had to be very careful not to fall or break bones because my cancer tends to make them much weaker. And there is a much longer time required for healing. So the beautiful hill from the driveway to the house on the pond that we had admired in the leaves of reds, browns, and yellows when we had arrived was now treacherous with a coating of snow and ice. I had fallen several times already and noticed that the bruises took a lot longer to heal than several years ago.

One cold gray morning, we were out driving picking up groceries at Stop & Shop and medicines at CVS. We passed by the same sign that we always see heading to our house … 'Route 495 South / Cape Cod.'

"David, let's go to Provincetown. The last time we were there it was hot and sunny and full of tourists. Now it should be less crowded."

Shin's voice echoed with excitement … as usual, she was trying to cheer me up. I knew that, so I agreed that this was a great idea.

"Let's go. We haven't had fresh seafood for many months — I can taste the fried clams already."

We headed out to the tip of the Cape in the Atlantic Ocean, watching as the trees changed from tall and majestic to short and wind-blown. The sides of the roads went from black earth to yellow sand as we proceeded East. The ocean side had large splashing waves, the bay side had quiet, icy, still water.

When we got to Provincetown, we walked up and down the main street with the shops, restaurants, the library, and the town hall. Almost everything was closed for the season. Many had signs that said 'See You Next Spring'. The town seemed eerily deserted. The bite of the frigid weather seemed to create a quiet gloom.

A few local people busied about their errands, not thinking about entertaining tourists now. There were a half-dozen commercial fishing boats active on the pier.

"What kind of fish are you after?" I asked.

"Mostly swordfish," a guy with yellow rubber coveralls answered. "Last week's unusual snowstorm here stirred up the water pretty good. We're hoping there's some fish in the aftermath."

He was coiling ropes on his boat ready for another try the next day. There were no fishermen on the other boats although they all seemed ready to go at a moment's notice if a boat out at sea sent a hopeful radio message.

We were getting hungry so we started looking for open restaurants. Most of the ones that we had eaten at in the summer were closed for the season. We walked into one possibility but it was actually mostly a bar and the special was pork chops. I had my heart set on seafood for lunch so we walked on.

Eventually Shin noticed a place at the beginning of the pier with the fishing boats. I was skeptical.

"I think they just sell coffee, cookies, and salt water taffy."

She pulled at my arm, "Well let's look anyway."

I was wrong. The menu showed fried clams, shrimp, scallops, haddock, and French fries as well as clam chowder and lobster bisque.

There was only one other couple in the restaurant so the waitress came right over. We split a "fisherman's platter" — a taste of almost everything — and put lots of salt on the French fries. The seafood lunch was excellent, a bit of sunshine in an otherwise desolate day.

"David, remember that tower that you can climb to the top of and see for miles? Let's go there again after we finish this lunch

... it will be good exercise for you. I've never been to the top since it's always been closed before. I mean you don't have to go all the way up, just try to go as far as you can. Dr. Portinari mentioned that you were gaining weight because the steroids make you hungrier so you have to balance that off with more physical activity."

"Ok, sure, that tall stone tower that you can see from everywhere. It's made of granite and called the Pilgrim Monument — it's a replica of a tower in our favorite country, Italy."

I knew there was no way that my body would make the 200 steps to the top. But why ruin Shin's fun? It would probably take her less than ten minutes.

When we got there, the door was locked, the entry lobby was empty and a sign said 'Closed for the Winter Season.' Shin shrugged off the minor failure,

"Ok, let's head off to the beach. We'll go up next time."

I breathed a sigh of relief. "Yes my darling, that will be perfect." But plans for next time always hurt ... especially when I say them to my Shin. I still did not know how many promises I could not keep.

Then we headed a mile away to Race Point beach, at the tip of the Cape. We parked in the lot near a small white lighthouse and walked along the beach. Endless sand dunes in both directions were partly covered by wildly waving dune grass.

Weathered brown wood fences attempted futile control of the constantly shifting sands — now they held small patches of ice and snow. The beaches were covered with a blizzard of windblown sand. It hit our faces hard, stinging in a way that feels good for only a moment.

It was impossible to walk directly into the wind. The towering waves crashed into the shore sending salt water droplets into our mouths even though we were a hundred yards away from the water. Just like my situation now, I thought, facing a powerful cancer that had the strength and ferocity to destroy my life.

Then we headed for home.

All in all, it was a melancholy deserted day, but I felt a mysterious pull inside to hang on longer fighting cancer. It was as if the ocean spray contained special medicine. And I so much needed to climb the tower with Shin ... next time.

Then the darkness swallowed us up before we got to the house. It seemed that we wanted time to pass but also wanted to point to some type of accomplishment. So the trip to Provincetown was just right. We were restless but content as we waited for the doctors to decide what to do next.

Some nights, we would listen to Bach cello suites and play Scrabble. Shin likes the game because it teaches her spelling and new words as well as the difference between regular words and proper nouns like Wells Fargo and Costco.

"David, is 'quoz' a word?"

"No way, that would win the game for you. Lucky for me it's not a real word."

"I'm sure I've seen it before. Where's the dictionary?"

"No, that must be 'quiz' you're thinking about. That is like a short test that a teacher gives school kids sometimes."

"Oh, okay," as she reached over to rub my neck. Her smooth hand felt like silk, comforting me.

But the soft structured Bach cello music seemed to echo a deeper warning of things not yet done.

Shin read my thoughts, "You're still worried about the money to take care of me next year, aren't you?"

"Of course, I'm not just worried about the money but I do want to provide you with great opportunities and challenges and exciting adventures, whether I'm here or not."

"Don't worry, I've been poor before, I can survive. Look where I got to from my days as a young girl. In elementary school every year there was a school picnic where kids brought their own lunch with a bottle of favorite soda from home. But me and my friend had no money to buy such luxuries and rather than be embarrassed, we always skipped the picnic ... every single year. Instead, we went and played by the river near our house. I still remember how sad we were."

The Bach cello music turned slow and somber while Shin studied her scrabble pieces to assemble her next word. Her legs were nicely tucked cross-legged under her in a comfortable position that I could not duplicate. Her orange t-shirt covered the dark blue soft shorts that she had on to wear to bed. Her brow furrowed and she continued her story.

"Many years later I heard that my childhood friend was very sick in the hospital. She was dying of some sort of cancer, though she was still very young in her early thirties, and had two kids. I went to visit her and she was yelling at the nurses, doctors, and her husband because she felt that she was just too young to die. I bundled her up in her coat and took her out on a trip to the river where we had played as young girls. We sat on a blanket and cried and rested and enjoyed nature. My friend said it was the best day she had all year. Soon after that, there was the funeral."

Some nights I cannot sleep. Sitting in my favorite chair, I look at my collection of books and classical music CDs. On the right across the room is a chair we use to store clothes we've already worn but will wear again. To my near left is a table with a camera, a glass of cranberry juice, and a lamp.

To my far left, Shin smiles. She is the queen of the bed. I watch her pretty face, eyes closing, *"Jaja* ... lets sleep" she says as she dozes off. Instead, I watch the black windows on the pond.

But another guy sits across from me typing on a computer. Can he watch over Shin when I'm gone? She needs someone to open her life to new things. To thank her for great cooking, to drop her at the health club for a sauna, to tease her about eating chocolate candy, to kiss and hug her for hope, to give her hints when she is at the computer, to listen to her stories about people and feelings.

Who will do this for me?

Will the guy in the window do this?

No, he cannot help. He goes with me. Shin sleeps, I cry inside.

———

One morning, the snowflakes drifted lightly from the sky, turning the window into an emptied pillow of white feathers. We snuggled in the warmth of the living room.

"David, does this cancer ever make you feel sad or depressed?"

I moved closer to her on the couch and held her hand. I hesitated.

"I feel bad that we can't do all the traveling that we planned and that my old career is over. Plus, as you know the chemotherapy medications sometimes create a chemical depression that lasts for several days every month."

"More than that, I mean ... "

"But when you are here and the effects of the medicine are light, I feel pretty good. We have a lot of fun doing things together and there doesn't seem to be any reason to mope around." I thought for a moment how to say what I knew she was really asking ... about death.

"Sometimes if I start to feel depressed, I catch myself and remember that I may not have many months to talk and play with you and read books, take walks, work on my computer, and watch movies. Suppose it is only two years. Why should I spend the little time I have left feeling sorry for myself?"

She wiped her eyes and then smiled.

"That's the kind of spirit it takes to deal with cancer ... you're so brave."

"Not really. Maybe I'm starting to believe in reincarnation ... 'Death is just a boundary between the end of one life and the beginning of another.' On days that I really accept that, I'm not so concerned about the poison in my blood."

I felt stronger then, so I tickled her playfully.

"How about let's go for a walk in the snow."

———

As the weather grew colder, Shin adopted the habit of taking me on a drive at least once a day to get out of the house and entertain me with the scenes of daily life passing by. One Sunday afternoon before Christmas, as we drove by downtown Milford we spotted a sign for a presentation of Handel's Messiah at the oldest church in town.

From the outside, it was a typical Gothic stone church that was copied from those built in the Middle Ages in Europe. It could be seen for miles because it had a tall square stone bell tower attached that reached over a hundred yards into the sky. Inside there were seven arches and six stained glass windows depicting stories from the bible on each side of the church.

Special lights at night made the reds, blues, and yellows of the stained glass shine like colored sunshine over the dark oak pews. A choir loft over the entry held a huge pipe organ and the stone ceiling arched overhead about fifty yards above the church altar.

Shin noticed that the concert was just about to start,

"Come and sit, let's listen David ... please?"

"Of course. I love that music as well. This is good. This is good."

The choir wore red and black robes with green sashes and the forty person orchestra was dressed in classical black suits and dresses. The majesty of Handel's tribute to the Christmas story was awe-inspiring and full of hope and triumph.

For the first time in weeks, Shin and I felt clouds lifting from our hearts. The stirring rendition of voice and music seemed to release a quiet anticipation of much better things to come

When the choir had finished, Shin was beaming with joy. "David, this is one of my favorite classical music compositions. When I worked at the textile mills when I was a young girl, most people just heard the whirring and grinding and clunking of the various machines.

"Not me. I was listening to the different voices of Handel's Messiah — first tenor, then bass, then alto, then soprano ... all blending into a marvelous combination with the orchestra."

She glowed, proud of her musical talent.

"People wondered why I sometimes waved my arms like a choir director at the textile mill."

For the reception after the concert, volunteers had made hot chocolate and cut-out Christmas cookies shaped like stars and candy canes. The smell of evergreen wreaths brought back pleasant memories of Christmas from years ago as we complimented the musicians and singers and met some new people from town. Smiles and warmth and love seemed to overcome all the troubles and doubts that surrounded us.

A five year old girl with curly blond hair and a brand new red and green dress ran wildly across the foyer dodging among the reception guests, "Mommy mommy, I get to be the angel in the

Christmas play!" Grinning widely, she was delighted to be one of the stars of the upcoming show.

Shin and I smiled at her good fortune.

We walked out into the cold night air, refreshed and renewed, with "For unto us ..." echoing in our heads.

Shin zipped up her jacket, "This is a nice European-like church ... we should come back again. St. Mary of the Assumption. I guess Mary refers to the mother of Jesus, but what does Assumption mean?"

"Well the Catholics believe that Mary didn't really die like a normal person. She was just standing in the right place and was whooshed up into heaven when it was her time to go. That's what I hope happens to me. Whoosh ... no pain ... no teary goodbyes ... no long drawn out months of agony. Just whoosh."

"Please Shin, don't be sad when it happens."

She turned away to bite her lip and hide a tear. I knew what she was doing. We didn't talk much as we drove home.

We were still trying to get used to the heart-wrenching confusion about whether to be happy or sad.

God's Plan

"David, guess what I'm making today … a Korean sweet soup called *dan pat juk.* It has red beans and dumplings made of rice flour all in a sugar sauce. You will love it."

"Great, I haven't had anything sweet for weeks."

"This is not an ordinary dessert … this is very special. My mother used to make it every Christmas Eve to serve to church people when they finished singing Christmas carols. Our house was the last one they did and they were cold and hungry. But as they arrived, they smiled and laughed when they saw my mother with the nice hot sweet soup. She was such a good person … I'm sure she is in heaven."

Shin walked out of the kitchen to the armchair where I sat.

"When I smell the red bean soup, I miss my mother so much …I wish she were here now. I would tell her how much I love her. I never said that enough when she was alive. But I know now it's too late."

She started singing a sad plaintive Korean song, *"ne gassum ey …."*

"That's nice. What does it mean?"

"The words are 'from my heart.' It's a song about someone missing the one they love."

"It sounds so beautiful. I should record it some day."

She seemed melancholy so I hugged her to try to cheer her up.

She continued, "My mother was so poor most of her life, but she was never sad or depressed … she never lost hope. And she always found a way to give money to others and to the church. At dinner, she even saved rice for the homeless people who came by the house afterwards, even though she was still hungry. She spent her whole life helping others. Now I want to give something back to her, but I can't because she's gone."

I listened to Shin quietly.

"I remember one very happy time with my mother after I got married. She came to visit me in Busan in the south of Korea and we went to the farmer's market together to shop. Busan is on the sea so there was a huge fish market there too. When my mother saw the tables of cod, anchovies, and squid right off the boats, she seemed so happy. We bought a couple of nice fish, some radishes, and a bunch of green onions for dinner.

'It's going to be a nice meal for the whole family,' I said excitedly.

'Sure, it'll be good, but I need some more.' she said.

'Ok, what would you like to buy?' I wondered.

'What about the fish over there?' She asked.

'Sure, how many do you want?'

'How about five boxes?'

She pointed to a cart of brown wooden boxes ... each container had about fifteen to twenty codfish packed in ice.

'Mother,' I looked at her in shock. 'Who will eat all that?'

Then she turned to me and said,

'The last time I visited you, I met two thin-looking eight year old girls ... they were so beautiful. As I talked to them, I learned that they lived in an orphanage, not very far from your house. If you can afford that much, they can all have a nice fish dinner too ... just like us.'

I didn't even know that there was an orphanage near the house. But now I knew why she wanted so many fish.

'Sure, we can buy it but we'll have to take a taxi home just to carry it all.'

I was relieved and happy that she could give all this to the orphans and didn't have to worry about the money to pay. I felt good that I could help her even though it wasn't very much. She deserved it."

I whispered, "It sounds like she was a wonderful person."

Shin wiped her eyes and continued reminiscing.

"One day she told me 'Be the best mother you can. Devote your life to Ejin and Ehang until they are grown up. I tried to do that for you, but as you know, there are lots of things that I wanted to do but I couldn't.' I'll never forget the day she told me that."

I reached out to hold her hand in silence while her mind wandered with thoughts of her mother and her daughters.

We watched the window as white flakes began to fall.

After a while I spoke. "Look, it's snowing again — I guess we'll have a white Christmas this year."

"That's nice."

But she was thinking about something else.

"Life is so wonderful with you now, David ... even though you still have cancer. I feel so comfortable and content. Don't you feel that way too?"

"Yes, definitely. I'm so thankful that we are together."

She held my hand tightly.

"Is it Ok to go to Korea sometime next year? I need to see my two daughters and tell them more about their grandmother ... how wonderful and generous she was. I also want to tell them to 'be the best mother they can' when they have their own children ... just like my mother told me. Are you healthy enough to stay alone for a couple of weeks?"

"Of course. Please go whenever you need to. I'll be fine. Next month, I should be much healthier."

Actually I had no reason to be so hopeful. But today it seemed Ok to make promises. After all, it was almost Christmas.

The snow continued to fall, coating the trees, houses, and roads with a smooth white mist. Everything seemed frozen in time in an icy picture of white and gray. Yet we were warm and cozy in our own special world.

Later that day, Shin drove to the health club in town for some time in the sauna while I rested at home. An icy rain was falling on top of several inches of snow. City snowplows had just started to spread sand and salt.

After my nap, it was dark. The icy rain had stopped and the trees were bent over from weight of the wet snow. I decided to surprise her by preparing supper before she got here. I made her favorite American meal … apples, pears, cheddar cheese, brie, and a French baguette. Then I began to wonder where she was.

―――――――

In the hospital waiting room later, the doctor said,

"The accident was pretty serious. A large semi-trailer truck skidded in the snow and totaled your car and hurt Mrs. Shin very badly. We did everything we could to try to save her. She died about ten minutes ago. You can go in and see her."

I froze in terror. "Oh my God!"

I stood there blankly.

The nurse touched my shoulder gently, "It's Ok to go in."

I entered the stark white hospital room in tears. Shin lay in the bed as peaceful and serene as a beautiful angel. She seemed to be smiling in her sleep. I couldn't even call her name or hold her … the only movement in that white room was tears coming down my face and onto my shirt. Her face was as pretty as ever, just like the pictures I had taken of her in the summer sun in Italy. The rest of her body was covered with a white sheet.

I was crushed. I couldn't breathe. My Shin is gone forever. I will never ever be able to play and talk with her again. I will never again feel the warm touch of her hand on my arm. Never.

She once told me 'When God calls, I will say, yes sir, here I am. I'm ready.' I can still hear her sweet confident voice.

North Pond Dawn

———————

At home these days, I peer out the window looking for the brown house across the pond. Shin is probably happy and warm there in her new home with her mother. But here, thick white snow blankets the trees in a lonely cold. Each morning, I sadly watch the frozen dawn over North Pond come and go. But I always smile about my happy life with Shin.

Acknowledgements

I owe a huge debt of gratitude to my family, nurses, doctors, counselors, and friends who have helped me adjust to my cancer and continue with my life.

A very special thanks to the light and hope and strength of my life, Song Bok Soon, who has been an insightful contributor to this book.

The brilliant editorial team of Song Bok Soon, Theresa Gorman-Kahler, Jin Young Lee, and Kelley Kavanagh helped make this book a reality in record time.

Medical Note

The medical information in this book is impressionistic. For official information, the following websites are a good start:

Dana Farber Cancer Institute
http://www.dfci.harvard.edu
Mayo Clinic
http://www.mayoclinic.com
U.S. Government National Institutes of Health
http://www.cancer.gov
American Cancer Society
http://www.cancer.org
Multiple Myeloma Research Foundation
http://www.multiplemyeloma.org
The Wellness Community
http://www.wellnesscommunity.org
The Leukemia & Lymphoma Society
http://www.leukemia-lymphoma.org

About the Author

David Roddy has written extensively about the world's telephone and Internet companies for thirty years. This book records his experiences since he learned that he has incurable cancer last year. He lives in a rustic cabin on North Pond in central Massachusetts.

For further information, please visit www.northponddawn.com .